John & Vivian
Thanks so much
your kindness.
Keep Dreaming
Enjoy!
Russ Phillips

MW01577715

Kneading a Dream

A novella

J. Russ Phillips

with Rachel McDonnell and Tabea Gietz

Copyright © 2008 by J. Russ Phillips

All rights reserved. No part of this publication may be reproduced, stored in a retrieval system or transmitted, in any form, or by any means, electronic, mechanical, recorded, photocopied, or otherwise, without the prior permission of the copyright owner, except by a reviewer who may quote brief passages in a review.

This book is a work of fiction. Names, characters, places and incidents are products of the author's imagination. Any resemblance to actual events or persons, living or dead, is purely coincidental.

Printed in the United States of America

ISBN: 978-0-6151765-8-1

In memory of Cathy Phillips, a loving wife, mother and prolific reader. Thank you for setting the standard of a book worth reading.

Acknowledgments

*To Rachel McDonnell, whose wit and energy can be felt on
every page. You have made your father very proud.*

*Tabea Gietz, thank you for making the story work on so many levels.
Thank you for sharing your mind and your heart.*

*Faith Farthing at FinalEyes Communications, thank you for
binding this team together and being much more than an editor.*

*To my wife, Jacque, who has added so much love
and support to this project and to my life.*

*Most importantly, to all of us frustrated dreamers,
may this story remind us that we are not alone.*

Chapter 1

Déjà Food

Habit is the denial of creativity
and the negation of freedom;
a self-imposed straitjacket
of which the wearer is unaware.
—Arthur Koestler

THE AIR IN THE HALL was filled with a strange miasma of processed cheese, deep-fried dough balls, and caramel corn; it was like a Halloween party that had ended badly. "Stay out of the way!" the 20-something kid shouted at Burton before continuing down the conference center hallway, pushing a stainless steel food cart at breakneck speed. In the seconds before Burton and the cart collided, he had been trying to stuff a six-ounce sample pouch of emulsified soy extenders into his Frito Lay tote bag, a "special gift" to anyone attending the Greater Chicago Snack Exposition. He had been gingerly trying to keep his just-purchased coffee upright at the same time. Now, he stood in the middle of the hallway, his front drenched by a large, half-caf, low-fat, extra-hot cappuccino. He cursed under his breath and then sighed heavily. The entire three-day conference had seemed like a series of disasters. *Why not add one more?* He just didn't care anymore.

Burton stooped to gather his empty cup and the scattered contents of his bag. One by one, he collected the candy, chips, and other snack samples, mechanically dropping them into the tote. He stopped to read the list of ingredients on the last bag. *This is what people are putting into their bodies?* Already, he was a little queasy from having sampled a wide assortment of salted, sweetened, dipped, roasted, and oven-baked tidbits. He felt his gut begin a slow, growing protest. *When will I learn? Year 15 of the Snack Expo, and I'm still down for the count by the end.* Burton looked for an escape.

Still thirsty but wary after being doused with coffee, he stopped to buy some bottled water and was aghast at the five-dollar price tag. *Should I really be surprised?* His stomach grew more and more unruly, and his legs ached from standing and walking for hours. With the optimism of a lottery ticket holder, he scanned a group of nearby chairs, looking for a seat. Finally, he was having some luck. There was a lone seat and, if he timed it right, he could claim it. Three long strides and he was there. Relief! He sat down and pulled out his bottle of antacids, his most trusted companion at the annual expo.

Popping an antacid into his mouth, he stared blankly into the milling crowd. This visit to the Snack Expo felt just like the 14 times before. After this final two hours of relentless snack-related déjà vu, he was looking forward to going home. The conference hall was cheery and bright—full of eager, smiling faces with snacks to peddle to unsuspecting passersby. Hundreds of men and women were there with their best game faces on. Burton didn't feel cheery or bright. He had heartburn. He popped another antacid into his mouth and loosened his bright pink and orange tie. He knew he must look ridiculous—stained and dressed in garish company colors.

"Hey Burton, how's it going?" A grating voice snapped him out of his thoughts. "Looks like you tangled with the wrong barista." Burton looked up. It was George, marketing vice president for one of the national potato chip companies, laughing at his own joke. Burton felt his stomach turn even more. George was obnoxious, always coming on strong about his brilliant ideas and novel product innovations. What was worse, like the school bully everyone hates, George seemed to delight in pointing out the failures of others. His achievements were always at the expense of someone else, and he took great pleasure in rubbing his success in people's faces. Burton winced as George fell into the recently vacated chair beside him.

"Can I have one of those?" George looked hopefully at Burton's antacids. "My wife told me to stay away from the nacho cheese puffs. Did I listen?" George leaned his head back and closed his eyes in mock agony.

"Apparently not." Burton handed George his near-empty antacid bottle. "But then, I'm in the same boat. The Scorcho Chips got me this time." Burton was trying, as he did every year, to lead with congeniality.

"Did you notice they stain your fingers red? You can't wash that crud off." George slowly chewed one antacid after another, looking off into the distance, emptying the tiny plastic bottle of all but two broken pieces. "I just polished off your stash," he said, handing back the bottle.

"No problem," Burton shrugged. "I've got more in my hotel room. I never come here unprepared. I always get heartburn at this thing. If they had any sense, they'd have an antacid booth at this show."

"Yup," George answered, simply. He let out a slow belch. "So...business as usual, Burton?"

"Business as usual, George." Burton knew what was coming.

"Well, things couldn't be better for me, Burton. We just launched a new french fry, our Freedom Fries. They're red, white, and blue."

"You found a market for blue french fries?" Burton could hardly believe what he was hearing.

"Hell, yes!" George exclaimed in triumph. "We shipped 120,000 pounds to the boys in uniform, just in time for the Fourth of July." Burton felt George's elbow dig into his side.

"And you did that for free, of course...out of the goodness of your heart." George seemed oblivious to Burton's sarcasm.

"You got it. Samples...just big samples is all. It's the least we can do to support the troops."

Burton couldn't help but be cynical. "Just how *did* the army embrace your new creation?"

This time, George's expression showed that he had clearly caught Burton's sarcasm. But he ignored it. "Those damn army cooks had the oil too hot, so the early batches came out kinda tan, red, and black. They look so pretty when they're frozen..." George said, almost wistfully. "It's a shame to have to cook 'em."

Burton broke George's reverie, "Tan, red, and black, huh? That's not a bad combination. Maybe back home here you can market them as Designer Fries." He couldn't help but smile.

"At least it's something new, Burton." George meant it as a barb, and it was. Burton's grip tightened around the antacid bottle. He knew he was stuck in a rut. He hated it, but he didn't know how to get out of it.

George smelled blood and went in for the kill. "What new ideas have you got going Burton? The only one with any fresh ideas is your wife. Now she's got her six health bars, and that's it. Burton's selling his 'lady bars,' same six flavors, year after year. Nothing ever seems to change at Hall's."

Burton was head of a company whose products targeted mainly women—health bars for the conscientious and active woman. Miss Munchie health bars had really been his wife Julie's dream. It was the only product line the company, Hall's Health Products, sold. Burton had helped her create a corporate culture that, to him, felt more like a theme park, with pixies, cutesy slogans ("Do lunchie with Miss Munchie"), Munchieville merchandise, all sporting the company's colors: sorbet versions of pink and orange. As a nutritionist, Julie knew health bars. As a woman, she knew how to appeal to other women. As an experienced businessman, Burton knew how to create, distribute, and sell product. As a husband, he knew how to support his wife and family.

"You ever think about selling something a *guy* could eat?" George prodded.

"Men are 17 percent of our market, you know. Actually, I'm pretty sure you *do* know, considering how many free samples you made off with last year," Burton reminded him.

"Says the man in the *pink* tie," George pressed. "A guy is bound to have serious masculinity issues eating a Miss Munchie Super Crunchie bar. You ever think how such a froufrou logo limits you?"

"I'm all for new ideas, but I want to make sure they're good ones and that they mean something. There are also a lot of other people to think about when it comes to launching a new product." It wasn't that Burton didn't want change. In fact, he was getting sick of the status quo. Right before George had come along, Burton had been daydreaming about the untimely and violent death of Miss Munchie. He was tired of his cartoonlike existence. Sometimes he wondered if there was a "happily ever after" apart from kids' stories. It all became just business as usual, day in and day out.

"What do you mean, 'There are a lot of other people to think about'?" George sounded incredulous.

"Well, don't you bounce these ideas off other people?"

"Not a chance! Nobody! This business is awash with Tater Tot terrorists waiting to steal from you and beat you to market."

Burton was taken aback by George's harsh outlook. "Not even your staff? You don't go to them for feedback?"

George bristled. "Hell, no! They're with you one day and peeling for the competition the next. It's every man for himself, Burton. Don't share a good idea with anyone. That's my motto."

"Wow, I guess it's smart to be careful, but it's hard to run a one-man show too."

George wasn't listening. "Designer Fries, huh? That's not bad, Burton. I've already got the product... Maybe we can do a little advertising on that fool home makeover network that has my wife addicted. Not bad. You know," George said, slapping Burton on the shoulder, "you should use that strategic thinking in your own business."

Burton didn't like George's patronizing tone. He didn't like his business philosophy either. Good ideas were one thing. Good execution was quite another.

Burton wondered if he was just making excuses for his own

KNEADING A DREAM 13

lack of innovation. Miss Munchie had always been Julie's thing. It had been quite a while since the company had introduced anything new. Julie didn't want to mess with a good thing. Profits were consistent. Burton felt a little guilty for even wanting more. *Why rock the boat? Still, I'd rather be in a speedboat than a rowboat. Shouldn't life feel more like an adventure?*

George stood up and stretched. "Well, it's been good to chat again, Burton. Next year, how 'bout you try to have something new to talk about?" He laughed, almost sneering. "Take care, Munchie Man." He slapped Burton on the shoulder again and disappeared into the throng.

Burton straightened his tie and decided he needed to get moving. But he couldn't seem to launch himself from the lobby chair. He slumped down even further, deflated by his exchange with George. Every year it was the same. He didn't want success or even the thrill of a new idea George's way. But he did envy the rush of having something new and exciting to pursue.

Burton noticed a woman, arms full of conference brochures, making her way toward him. *This must be Burnout Central,* he thought as he watched the slightly disheveled woman weave her way through the crowd to the row of chairs. She tossed her bag down on the floor and flopped inelegantly into the chair George had just vacated.

She cast a sideways glance at Burton. "I'm afraid to ask what's on your shirt," she said tentatively.

"Coffee," he said simply.

She looked relieved. "Antacids?" she asked with an optimistic sigh as Burton flipped his empty bottle. She kicked her heels under the chair. She looked tired and worn from the snack food frenzy.

"Sorry, I'm all out," Burton laughed. He tossed the bottle

into a nearby trash can. "Was it the Scorcho Chips? They should come with a warning label."

"I'm surprised I didn't need to sign some release of liability." She leaned over and extended a hand to Burton. "Susan Jenson. I'm with Brigham Airlines."

"Burton Hall of Hall's Health Products, more commonly known as Miss Munchie Health Bars."

"Well, that explains your tie," Susan laughed. "My daughter lives on those things. She's in high school...always in a hurry and already worried about her figure. You still have the cranberry and apple bar? That's my favorite."

"Same six flavors. My wife is the master chef, and she's been pretty happy with our original ideas. Not much passes her test-kitchen rigors."

"Why mess with a good thing, huh?"

"I guess so," Burton looked down at his tie. "We've established a tradition now, I suppose."

"So has Brigham Air, but not the good kind." Susan glanced at her messy canvas bag full of brochures. "Our tradition is terrible in-flight food."

"Hey, don't be too hard on yourself now. Every airline has bad food—or no food at all." He was trying to make her feel better, though he felt like the last person qualified to offer a positive perspective.

"Proud tradition, isn't it?" Susan smiled at him. "That's why I'm here; I'm looking for something that might help us improve our food service. I'm afraid all I've found are junk food and indigestion."

"Well this *is* nutritional ground zero. Not much here will help you improve your reputation. Just curious... What kind of products were you hoping to find?" He felt a little guilty thinking that it was refreshing to hear of someone else's search for something new. Maybe Susan could offer some hope.

"I'm not sure it exists," Susan said thoughtfully as she looked out over the lobby. "We need something that is more than a snack but lighter than a full meal…something we can serve easily and at low cost…not a sandwich or another typical airline feed bag. I don't know, really, but Brigham needs something that will really please its customers. I'm sure I haven't seen it yet."

You and me both. "Interesting." Burton couldn't help but think of the many products he'd seen and sampled today. Nothing quite fit Susan's description. "I'm not sure you're going to find what you need here. Lately, the focus in the industry has been on the youth market—not really the kind of food you'd see favored by business travelers."

"Exactly." Susan rubbed her feet and sighed, bracing herself to dive back into the throng. "Well, Burton, if Miss Munchie ever ventures into airline service, give me a call. Of course, we have to serve both men and women," she laughed. "I'm not sure the pink and orange would go over well with our male passengers."

"Probably not," Burton said, shaking his head, "but you would be number one with teenage girls."

Susan smiled as she stood and heaved her canvas bag over her shoulder. "We both know how much that demographic travels! I'd better get back out there. Brigham is adamant that I not come home empty-handed."

"You know," Burton ventured, "I'm intrigued by this airline food service angle. May I have one of your cards? I wouldn't mind thinking seriously about developing a product."

"Sure. Absolutely!" Susan handed Burton her card and slipped her heels back on. "I'll tell you up front that we're talking serious dollars here, Mr. Hall. We're willing to work on an exclusive basis...shared development expenses...whatever. This is a potential $14-million-per-year opportunity for someone with the right ideas. Let me know." Burton felt his mind already starting to race. "Nice to meet you, Burton," Susan finished, offering her hand and shaking his.

"Same here," he replied. "Good luck out there, and I hope to be in touch."

Burton looked at the business card and let his mind wander as Susan walked back into the heart of the conference center. He reached into his briefcase and pulled out a tattered, leather-bound notebook. It was his diary, several years old now and well-worn with use. He took it everywhere he went, almost as an extension of himself. He flipped through it casually. Page after page was covered with his excited scrawl, idea after idea—some business and some more personal—that had, at one time or another, got his heart racing and his mind going. He was halted by something he'd written a few years ago: "Airline food. Tasteless meals. Poor snacks...stale. Need something convenient but tasty as a meal or meal supplement. New snack bar?" That was as far as he'd gone. That's as far as any of his ideas had gone. Written down and then, in the course of days or weeks, abandoned.

Now he wondered at the significance of having met Susan here, today, in this circumstance. *Is there any point to this, Burton? Do you dare venture outside Munchieville?* Still, it felt good to run with something new, even if only for a few moments. George's jabs came back to him. The man was hard to take, but he was right. Burton hadn't come up with anything new, not really. What if there really was something to this airline idea? Maybe it would be his turn to report to George next year.

He closed the diary and turned it over and over in his hands, feeling the softness of the leather, reflecting on how much of his life was between those leather covers but dormant. Revived by ideas that were not wrapped in the pink and orange packaging of Munchieville, Burton slipped the diary back into his briefcase and headed back into the din of the conference center.

Chapter 2

"Just Sell Them Bars, Boy"

*A mind troubled by doubt
cannot focus on the course to victory.*
—Arthur Golden

THE HOTEL BUS WAS AMBLING slowly through traffic. Burton watched the pouring rain and the long line of cars winding ahead. Leaning his head against the cool of the window, his thoughts drifted back to his conversation with Susan. Weren't the best business ideas the intersection of a real need and a great product? She had presented the need, and, given his experience with airline service, he knew it was valid. *What if I could help meet that need and create that product? Could this be the something new I've been looking for?* He felt the boat beginning to rock—and he liked it.

In an instant, he was back at the Goo Bar factory some 30 years ago, thinner, younger, eager, and poised for a business adventure. *I don't remember that guy*, thought Burton. He pictured his father, king of the famous Goo Bar, a candy bar the confectionary patriarch developed in the early '50s and sold until the day he died. Nothing would have made his father prouder than if Burton had taken over the family business, protecting his precious Goo Bars for future generations.

When Burton had been a child, his father's company had seemed so complex and...magical. He grew up helping on the factory line, working every summer beside his dad. By the time he was 15, he knew the Goo Bar plant and processes inside and out. But alongside his business savvy, Burton's disillusionment with his father's dream was growing and becoming burdensome. He knew the company was an aging relic of another time—a candy-coated dinosaur—and that his father was a committed preservationist, determined never to change the product. The company offered a candy bar with or without peanuts. Period.

Once he completed college, Burton couldn't imagine devoting his life to his father's sticky candy creation. Burton was different. He wanted more. He wanted his work—his life—to matter. *What a joke,* he thought, lifting his head from the bus window. *Dad had two flavors. I have six. Big deal, Munchie Man. You're no different.*

When his father passed away, his mother was shocked to hear Burton suggest selling the company. "It's what we *do*, Burton. How can we trust anyone else with your father's company?" Her disappointment was heavy and oppressive that day and for many that followed; it was like another death. He sympathized with her, but he knew she was never going to see reality. He didn't want to tear down what she embraced as his father's legacy, but he knew there wasn't much, if anything, to build his own career on.

Ultimately, after much haggling, the family sold the company to a huge corporation, Global Foods. Burton's mother was grateful for the income and security, and she felt some illusion of control despite the business having changed hands. During negotiations, she made sure Global Foods had the original Goo Bar recipe, written out as precisely as her husband's first record. She adamantly refused to finalize the deal unless she could personally speak with the new owner. Burton recalled the day of that meeting, when his petite, 85-year-old mother, dressed in a soft pink sweater and her best pearls, leveled the Global Foods CEO a ferocious, iron gaze. She leaned on her walker and pointed menacingly, "Do. Not. Change. A thing." She was like a queen that day, her shoulders square, her voice steady.

After the verbal promises were made and the written deal was signed, the large conglomerate quickly dismantled the aging Goo Bar plant, dropping the family legacy like an old candy wrapper. Burton felt a pang of guilt as he remembered that moment. He had known better—that Global Foods would take the name and image and discard everything else. Yet he had watched his mother go through her impassioned speech. He had truly believed he was doing the right thing, the best thing for her financially. But in the years since, he had wrestled with the guilt of having dashed her dreams and betraying his father's hope for his legacy. With everything in him, Burton had believed he was breaking a new trail, creating his own adventure that day—something that was his own, something that was real, and something that was big enough to matter. Now here he was on a bus at a conference that was exactly the same as the conference before, sporting a sickly sweet tie—one of several in his well-organized closet. Some adventure. *I didn't take a new road. I am on the same beaten path as my father. At least he enjoyed it. At least he believed in what he was doing.*

His parents had been proud of their product but always fearful of the future and of change. Steeped in old-school thinking, his father had believed in simple plans and hard work. "Just sell them bars, boy," Burton could still hear him say. "Just sell them bars. That's all you need to worry about. The product will do the rest." Every change Burton suggested was summarily rejected; every proposal was analyzed until it met its inevitable withering and painful demise. Time and again, Burton had approached his father with ideas, suggestions to produce a lighter bar or a new flavor, with hopes of slowing the now-steady decline in sales. He was itching to see something new, something alive and growing—some kind of excitement for a change. "Goo Bars got us where we are, and they're gonna take us where we're going," his father had said, confidently oblivious.

That stifling predictability was what had ultimately prompted Burton to start his own company. When he married his wife, Julie, she was finishing her degree in nutrition. Goo Bars horrified her. To her they were a fat-laden dietary disaster. She had been so excited when the two of them decided to start their own business. Fresh-faced and full of ideas and dreams of her own, she was the driving force behind what had begun as her simple recipe for breakfast bars but had quickly transformed into a thriving business. Burton remembered the way Julie, who had always avoided Goo-related topics, suddenly peppered him with questions and brainstormed new business ideas at the dinner table. She had even helped him commandeer Charlie, then their only child, to help in the test kitchen. Thankfully, Charlie's Peanut Butter and Potato Chip Surprise bar had never gotten past the concept stage. Now they had their 17-year-old son, Charlie, their 10-year-old daughter, Samantha, and a six-bar lineup—Miss Munchie health bars. Julie's enthusiasm for her new product had been catching, and, full of love and devotion for his wife, Burton was content to make her dream his. Back then. *Just sell them bars, boy. Just sell them bars.* The voice was the same, but now it came from his own mind. He was the same. *It's all the same.*

After the bus pulled up in front of the hotel, Burton slogged his way up to his room. Staring out the rain-splashed window, he made a few calls to the office and began booting up his laptop, hoping to knock off a few e-mails so he could relax. He called home, wanting to hear his wife's voice. Julie answered with her usual sunny "Hello." Right away, the sound of her voice made Burton smile. He adored her. She was still his light. "Julie, I am so glad to hear your voice. How are things going? I can't wait to get home."

"It's crazy here, as usual. How was the conference?" She sounded excited, like he ought to have had the time of his life. But, of course, he hadn't.

"It's business as usual here. I've got heartburn, and I feel like a dork in a pink and orange tie."

"I love your tie!" Julie laughed. She was consoling. "You always get grumpy at that conference."

"As I recall, so do you," said Burton. Most years, the two of them attended together. But things were busy at home with their kids' school and extracurricular activities, and she was minding things at the office. "Thanks for delegating," Burton teased.

"Something good always comes out of it, honey. Try to perk up."

He wondered if she felt herself trying to cheer him up more often lately. He wanted to share the one thing at the conference that really had piqued his interest, but he was hesitant. How would his wife react? Despite feeling cautious, he ventured anyway. "I actually ended up talking to a VP over at Brigham Air. They're looking for something new to add to their food service.

We knocked around an idea for an airline meal a few years ago, remember?" He wanted her to meet him in his stirring interest.

"Vaguely," Julie answered. Burton could hear the steady tap of the keyboard in the background. He sighed. Julie was undoubtedly doing her usual three things at once. Burton waited silently through her distracted pause. She finally answered, "We didn't think that was a direction to pursue at the time. That's what I recall." Had she been waiting to answer, trying to choose her words? She still sounded pretty upbeat.

"Well, from what Susan, the vice president, was sharing today, I don't think we were too far off base. I think it may be time to think that idea through a little further. Looks like it could be a good opportunity—as in $14 million annually and joint product development." Burton could hear Julie stop typing on the other end. Then it was just quiet.

"I wasn't aware we needed another opportunity. We're doing fine, and everything is running smoothly..."

"I know, Julie. We have a niche, a successful niche. But we've sold the same product for 15 years now. I think maybe it's a good time to start looking beyond Munchieville—to see if there's something else." Burton heard Julie's printer power up, and he waited again as she said something to her secretary.

"Sorry," she said. "What were you saying? You think we can get Brigham Air to distribute Miss Munchie bars on flights? Nice work, honey. That would be great!" *Just sell them bars, boy. Just sell them bars.*

Burton tried again, "No. They aren't interested in Miss Munchie bars...exactly."

"Well, then I don't understand. How do we fit in?" Julie's printer hummed in the background. "Oh darn," she said, fumbling with something. "Look, it's a bit busy just now. Can we talk when you get back? I'm not sure what you're getting at, but we have plenty keeping us busy, honey."

"Yeah. Just thinking out loud, Julie." That was it. Maybe he was just sharing his thoughts at the wrong time. Maybe they could talk things through when he got back home the next day and she wasn't in the middle of work. "I'll let you get back to work. Say hello to the pixies for me."

Julie laughed. "I'll pass that on. Remind me to show you the new pixie artwork for our lobby. It's too cute! See you tomorrow. I hope you don't get delayed flying home. Is the weather still bad?"

"It is. It'll be a small miracle if I'm not delayed. Keep your fingers crossed."

Burton said goodbye to Julie and sat on the edge of the bed, pulling his tie off. He thought about his wife's boundless energy and enthusiasm for the company. She reminded him of his father, focused and committed, but to Miss Munchie health bars instead of Goo Bars. *I'm always singing backup to someone else's song.* He knew Julie didn't mean to blow off his ideas; she just didn't see the need for anything else. His father had that same zeal, that same unwavering focus. And Julie was happy. She liked what she was doing. Burton had to concede that the business was working. Things were humming along nicely. Was it fair for him to want to shake things up, to potentially risk the stability—and success—they were enjoying? Still, Burton couldn't shake the feeling that he was the odd man out. His wife was happy, and he wanted her to be. But this was her dream, not his. He was the tired mayor of Munchieville in an ugly pink and orange tie.

As he sat and listened to the rain slash against the window, Burton imagined a world without pixie dust or Miss Munchie's pert, upturned nose. He picked up his diary from the bedside table. Flipping through it, he reminisced over old ideas and creative concepts. So much of his thought life was documented there. So much of *him* was laid out on those pages. Convinced that some of those long-abandoned ideas were precisely what Brigham Air was looking for, he let himself enjoy feeling inspired and began to chew on some new ideas.

Chapter 3

A Morning with Morty

> Millions long for immortality
> who don't know
> what to do with themselves
> on a rainy Sunday afternoon.
> —Susan Ertz

THE RAIN CONTINUED relentlessly through the night. As Burton made his way to the airport the next morning, the streets were teeming with grimy taxicabs depositing passengers at the terminal. Burton was the last passenger remaining on the small shuttle bus. Traffic wasn't even crawling anymore; he was stuck in a soggy gridlock, a few hundred feet from what he could see was a very busy terminal.

"Can I just get out here?" Burton asked, gripping his luggage. He was anxious to move. "I need to get going. That line is out the door." He scanned the crowd that had now pushed from inside the terminal out onto the wet sidewalk.

"I can't let you get out in this lane. I'll get a ticket, man. No one's goin' anywhere in this weather anyhow." The driver smiled wryly as he drummed the steering wheel to the steady beat of the windshield wipers. "The power was out last night. It's gonna be one hell of a mess in there."

Burton knew he was probably right, although he was annoyed at what almost sounded like enthusiasm. There was little chance of a timely departure, he knew. With a sigh, he waited until the bus maneuvered to the curb. He stepped off into a cold, murky puddle before pushing his way into the terminal. A sea of people surrounded him.

After a long wait at the check-in counter, Burton stood in the security line in his wet socks. His shoes and briefcase were slowly winding their way through the labyrinth of x-ray machines and security guards. The floor was bracingly cold on his wet feet. As he put his shoes back on, he surveyed the crowd and realized that most people had to be in the same state he was—tired, hungry, and anxious to be on his way. His gaze met many sour expressions. The flight board told the unwelcome truth, line by line: everything, including Burton's flight, was canceled due to severe weather. While weaving through the bustling airport, Burton had clung to the fleeting hope that escape might still be possible. Now, reading the flight board, his heart sank.

With a heavy sigh, he retrieved his bags and headed to the executive lounge. The much-touted exclusivity and service had clearly been abandoned in the face of the storm. The lounge was at full capacity. A harried hostess quickly scanned his card and offered a smile of helpless apology. "There aren't many seats open in there, but you might double-check to see if one's free."

Burton felt himself bristle as he scanned the crowded lobby. "I guess it's the *free* comment I take issue with. You guys charge a lot for this. I know it isn't your fault, but..." He stopped mid-sentence, realizing that she had already turned her hapless charms to the next person in line. He pushed his way through the lounge and to the coffee kiosk. The aroma of freshly brewed coffee after such a hectic, rainy morning was irresistible—a beacon of hope.

Moving cautiously into the dangerously under-caffeinated crowd circling the coffee kiosk, he hunted down a cup. Just when he had almost reached the coffee urn, the man ahead of him drained the last dregs into his cup. "Sorry, buddy," he said with no hint of remorse. "Looks like you'll have to wait for them to brew another pot." With a sigh, Burton begrudgingly filled his cup with decaf, which was—no surprise—still available. *Maybe this way I can sleep on the plane*, he thought, trying to look on the bright side, but he wasn't convinced. The decaf slopped over his hand as he looked for a seat.

"Looking for a place to sit?" a voice called from nearby. Burton saw three men sitting around a small table littered with coffee cups, muffin wrappers, and napkins. "Feel free to join us. We've got room for one more."

Burton felt some of the tension leave his shoulders. "Thank you. You don't know how much I appreciate this." He sank into the lone empty chair and placed what remained of his coffee on the table. The men continued their conversation, and Burton eased his chair slightly away from the chattering group. They were laughing with a younger man who seemed to be in the middle of a story.

"So, I bought one of those mocha-frappa-latte-whatever things and a bagel. I was starving, man, and that's all I could grab. I totally forgot I'd stuck the bagel in my boss's laptop case as I was boarding. I got cream cheese all over his laptop. I thought he was going to kill me!"

The men guffawed, and Burton felt himself relax a little

more, even savoring the bad coffee for the warmth it gave his cold hands, gripped around the cup. He felt a kind of kinship with the crowd—they were all suffering the same delays, setbacks, and annoyances.

"So, what do you do?" said a voice, jarring Burton back to reality. "I'm Morty, by the way, Morty Abrams." The tall man's New York accent and confident handshake made Burton feel at ease and welcome in this group of men. "Not sure who the rest of these bozos are," Morty laughed, as he gestured to his companions, "but they all seem to be on my payroll." The group rolled their eyes at what was apparently a much-used joke.

Burton shook Morty's hand and then the others'. "Burton Hall. My company makes the Miss Munchie health bars." Burton waited for the snicker that usually accompanied his association with Miss Munchie.

"My wife loves those things. Can't say I've tried them though, sorry." Morty flagged down a waitress. "This man needs a fresh cup of coffee, honey. He's already had a long day." Burton could tell by his easy, confident demeanor that Morty was a character and was used to calling the shots. Morty turned to Burton again, sizing him up. The gray eyes studied Burton's shirt and then moved to his face. "It seems to be a good product, Burton. Very successful. You guys have been around awhile, haven't you?"

"Fifteen years. We have a solid share of the health bar market. And we even covertly sell to *men*," he replied, giving a triumphant smirk over the rim of his coffee cup to the men at the table. "You know the saying: 'Real men eat Miss Munchie bars.'"

The group laughed easily, raising their coffee cups in a mock toast to Mr. Munchie. Burton was used to the teasing; he'd heard just about every joke there was about his pink and orange company. He gave a tired smile to the men and hoped the conversation would move to something else.

"Have you ever thought of selling the company?" asked Morty, his eyes narrowing.

I bet that's exactly what you'd do with it, Burton thought. *You'd have no problem burying Miss Munchie if it would bring you a tidy profit.* But for just a moment, Burton relished the thought himself. "My wife and I have kicked the idea around a few times. Never very seriously, though. How do you know when the time is right?" He wanted Morty to do more of the talking.

"When you're sick and tired of running the business," Morty grinned. He pulled out a business card and flipped it, like a Vegas dealer, to Burton. *Very slick*, Burton thought. "I'm an investment banker," Morty went on. "I'm always looking, you know. Give me a call if you ever want to get out of Munchie World."

"You mean Munchieville. The sign in our parking lot says, 'Welcome to Munchieville.'" Burton was making light, but there was something about this Morty character that made him want to hold his cards a little close. "I was thinking it might be time for change," said Burton, putting Morty's card in his pocket, "but I think it's about growing the company right now, not selling it off."

"Well, I find after 15 years, most CEOs are ready to get out. They want to spend more time with family and get away from the daily grind."

"And your daily grind is talking CEOs into selling out, huh." Burton chuckled, but wanted Morty to know he was savvy.

Morty slapped Burton on the back. "I shoot for two deals a month. And everybody's happy. You ought to at least think about it. What's the future look like for your company? Where are things shaking?"

"Not too much is shaking right now, but we've enjoyed slow and steady growth from the beginning. My wife developed a line of six products, and we've stayed true to that. We're doing about $30 million in annual sales." For some reason, Burton felt the need to let Morty know he was a success, that he was doing well. *It can't hurt to give him some round numbers*, Burton thought.

"Hmmm. I see." Morty scratched his chin and surveyed the room. "Investors look for potential growth, you know. Are you concerned at all that you might be pretty saturated within your market? You should think about that before you sell."

"Yes, but remember, I haven't been thinking seriously of selling in the first place." Burton was growing tired of Morty's inquisition. "Like I said, we kicked the idea around but haven't thought about it in ages."

"Hey, if you're happy, don't rock the boat, right?" Morty flashed Burton a slightly condescending smile. "Just be careful, Munchie Man. Fifteen years is a long time in any industry, especially yours. Food and drink trends change all the time."

Burton knew he was right. His mind wandered back to his conversation with Susan at the conference. "I may have something in mind."

Morty leaned back in his chair, mildly interested. "Oh yeah, what's that?"

"I'm considering working up an idea for the airlines." Burton felt a sense of triumph simply in talking about his idea out loud—even if it was to an old business shark like Morty.

"Tough market," Morty said, shaking his head slowly, "but plenty of room for improvement, that's for sure."

"I know. I've got plenty of legwork to do." Burton had to admit the airlines were going to be a hard group to please. So many things could go wrong in the industry; the scale was extraordinary and the obstacles as relentless as the storm raging outside O'Hare airport.

"Well, it helps to have something in play if you're thinking of selling it off too, you know. Hell, it helps to have something in play, period. People get bored and stuck in a rut, you know." Morty shot Burton a predatory look. "Of course, that's where I come in. I love a tired CEO. But that's not you, of course," Morty said, sneering slightly. He paused and then shifted in his seat. "I do know a guy, though. Mike Collier. He's a major customer service consultant for the airlines. He'd be a great guy to talk to." He scribbled down Mike's name and number and passed the slip of paper to Burton. "Give him a call if you're serious," Morty advised.

But that's not me, of course. I'm not a tired CEO. Burton felt mocked by Morty's comments, though he saw himself in them. But he took the contact information gratefully. *Was this a lead? Was something going to come of this airline thing? Did he dare to hope for a new adventure, or was he just spinning his wheels?* Morty and his posse ordered another round of coffee and flirted with the waitress.

He knew that introducing an idea, especially this one, to his staff and management team would be met with skepticism—if he wasn't shot down altogether. Julie and the Hall's staff had a protective inertia that made any kind of change daunting. Stability and status quo were safe and easy. Burton knew he had to think things through before he talked to the staff. He *wanted* to think things through. It felt easy and energizing to mull over this project. The adrenaline rush was a nice change from the predictable, stifling routine. It felt good just to *think* instead of react to the usual trivia that kept him occupied. *It's a lot more productive than fantasizing about killing Miss Munchie. It may be impractical, even crazy, but I want to work on this. I need something like this. Morty has one thing right: I'm in a rut. Fix it or sell it—but don't stay in the same place, Burton. Work on your own ideas for a change.*

Chapter 4

Getting off the Ground

We strain to renew our capacity for wonder,
to shock ourselves into astonishment once again.
—Shana Alexander

AFTER SEVERAL HOURS of waiting and a steady turnover of faces in the executive lounge, Burton was finally on his way home. As the plane lifted off the runway, he stared at his stowed tray table, wanting to snap it open and write down some of the ideas he'd had about an airline product. Normally, Burton would have focused on the flight itself—what seat he had been assigned or if he had managed an upgrade. Burton had a bad seat, he'd barely managed to board, and now he was nearly five hours late. But somehow he wasn't bothered. He was happy to have some uninterrupted, solitary time to think about his idea, and he was relieved to finally be on the plane.

The passengers were struggling to find space for bags, purses, and briefcases. He folded himself into his seat, jammed between a college student and an older man who, Burton quickly learned, was an overeager farm equipment salesman intent on handing out as many business cards as humanly possible before the flight took off. Burton knew making any eye contact would spark a minimum three-hour conversation, highlights of which would probably include the trials of finding good long-distance phone service and the man's struggles with sciatica. The student's earphones were set to a volume that would accomplish two concurrent goals: sharing his favorite tunes with the entire cabin and damaging his ear drums.

Despite the obstacles, Burton felt there was a lot he could do during the flight home; he could organize some of the ideas that were racing through his mind. As soon as the seatbelt light went off, he lowered his tray table and dug out his diary and a notebook. He flipped through the diary to find the place where he'd written some six years ago about the possibility of an airline product. Almost lovingly, he fingered the pages. *Where can I go with this?* He wasn't sure, but he knew he could no longer put off going down this road.

He knew better than to try to contain all his thoughts in the diary; it would take him no time at all to fill its remaining pages. Instead, he would record his summary thoughts and action items there. Before long, Burton had filled the notebook and a large stack of napkins. Every time he put his pen down, another thought would surface: ideas on product design, things he'd have to research, potential capital equipment costs, marketing ideas, and patent protection—among other things. Burton noticed the farm equipment salesman straining to see his notes. The burly man's curiosity was mounting with each additional napkin Burton scribbled on.

"You're pretty busy there. Where's the fire?" he finally asked.

"I'm just thinking through a few ideas—for work," Burton

replied, trying to be polite but also hoping to avoid further questioning. He glanced at his watch, noting to his surprise that nearly two hours had passed. He put down his pen. His fingers throbbed with a dull, cramped ache. He rubbed his eyes.

"You ain't thinkin', son. Looks like you're plannin'. Nice to see someone workin' for a change. On my last flight, the fella next to me played some card game on his computer for four hours straight."

"Yeah, it's actually nice to *be* working. I'm guilty of game addiction, though. I swiped a few of my son's video games awhile back and still haven't returned them. I'm a level eight wizard now, although I'm not sure that's really a good thing."

"Well, now I'm impressed. I figured all the wizards were up in first class." The man chuckled and took a sip of his near-empty drink. "It's easy to get sucked in. They're great distractions. Funny thing is, I already got plenty of distractions."

"Me too," Burton responded good-naturedly. He rubbed his eyes again and glanced down at his tray table, littered with notes. "Some distractions are better than others, I guess."

"That's for sure," the salesman laughed, as he pulled a box of Goobers from his briefcase. "Want a piece of today's special?"

"No, thanks. I'd hate to spoil my dinner. I'm sure I'll eat in about five hours."

The man reached down and grabbed his newspaper. "You better get back to your brainstorming. You're a man with a plan. Far be it from me to stall a guy making real progress. Good luck, son." With that, he turned to his paper.

Progress. Yes, I am making progress. Moving forward. I haven't felt momentum like this for a while. Burton fingered his pile of cards, thinking about airline passengers and the experience of flying. He knew the notes scattered on the tray table would begin to take shape and form a real strategy. He anticipated carving out a time when he could organize, clarify, and challenge his thoughts. But for now, he was content to be writing, doodling, and scribbling ideas—just brainstorming—letting old complacency be turned into new action.

Burton rang his call bell for the flight attendant. "I need a few more napkins, if you've got 'em," he said when she arrived.

"You need a notebook, you know," the stewardess smiled, handing Burton an ample supply of napkins.

"I know," Burton laughed, thanking her. "I've filled one already. Looks like I came on board unprepared."

"You may not have been prepared for the flight, but it sure looks like you'll be prepared for whatever it is you're working on there."

"You know," smiled Burton, "I think I will be." He nodded to himself and put pen to napkin.

Chapter 5

Touching Down

God is really only another artist; he
made the elephant, giraffe and cat.
He has no real style but keeps trying new ideas.
—Pablo Picasso

BURTON FINALLY LANDED in Los Angeles and was eager to see if his garment bag had enjoyed the same safe arrival. The passengers began collecting their things and shifting in their seats, eager to leave the cabin's confines. Outside, the sun was bright, and the sky was clear and warm, goading the passengers waiting in the stuffy cabin with promises of warm breezes just out of reach. Burton couldn't wait to take in fresh air. He was home, finally, and the Snack Expo was mercifully behind him, for another year anyway. Inside the terminal, waiting at the baggage carousel, Burton thought of his conversation with Susan and everything that had come out of that brief exchange. Now that he was home, he knew the challenge would be to maintain this momentum. He was already thinking of the next staff meeting, phone calls he needed to return, and countless other tasks that would clamor for his attention. He couldn't picture this messy stack of cards and napkins on his desk at work. Somehow they didn't fit there. Yet he couldn't give up hope of bridging those two worlds—the current success of the business and his emerging venture.

His mind went to Julie. Would Julie see it? Would she see that he was serious about this, that he really wanted to pursue it? Would she understand? Would she support him? Or would she try to shut him down? Would his staff see the potential? Who would be his allies, his enemies—or at least his roadblocks? *Am I really up for this?* He imagined himself on the golf course, swinging balls in a pink and orange polo shirt. *Yeah. I'm definitely up for this.* Burton was so lost in thought that when he finally turned his attention back to the luggage carousel, his battered bag was one of the last remaining. Smiling at his luck, he grabbed his things and hurried through the parking lot to his car, savoring that long-anticipated breath of fresh air.

Twenty minutes later, Burton pulled into his driveway. Willard, their wheaten terrier, came bounding up to him, panting with delight. Julie was wrist-deep in a flowerbed, one of her favorite places to be. Burton relished her smile. He waved as she greeted him. Her knees were muddy and her sunhat was threatening to slide off her head. Burton couldn't resist tugging the hat off as he kissed her hello.

"I am so glad to be home! You don't even know how glad," Burton said, hugging Julie tight.

"I think I'm getting some idea. *I'm* so glad you're home. The news said the storm was pretty bad."

"It was. The power was out at the airport last night. I was stuck at O'Hare since six this morning."

"I guess that explains why you look a little rumpled." Julie ran her finger lightly over Burton's scruffy chin. "I know you must be exhausted, but be warned. Charlie's been wheeling and dealing all afternoon. I think he managed to book you for some meeting this evening at the car dealer." She said this tentatively, studying his face.

Burton sighed, his shoulders collapsing. "You're kidding, right?" Then he spied Charlie peering out from behind his bedroom blinds. Waving madly, his eagerness and sunny enthusiasm belied his agenda.

Julie shot her son a warning look. She had been very clear with him that his father was going to be able to set his suitcase down before he heard the words "car," "dealership," or "co-sign."

"I need a shower and something to eat. Tell Charlie to exhale. He is *at least* a few hours away from ignition." He paused a moment before adding, "And I really want some time to talk to you about an idea I'm excited about."

"Sure, honey," she said. She seemed to sense how much Burton wanted to have that discussion. She looked him in the eye. "We'll have lots of time to talk, now that you're home." Brushing some dirt off her shorts, she said, "I'm going to clean up and then get some supper going. You must be famished."

"You have no idea," Burton replied.

Julie laughed and went inside. Burton scooped up his bags, stepped inside, and started to climb the stairs toward the bedroom and a hot shower. Charlie suddenly shot out onto the upstairs landing and came bounding down the staircase with an ebullient hello for his weary father.

"Dad! Wow, you're home! Heard you got stuck in Chicago."

Burton pictured an eager puppy. "Long trip, Charlie. Really."

He mussed his son's hair. "I'm glad to be back. It's been quite a day."

"Yeah, it's so cool you're home. I've been waiting for you." Burton laughed at his son's unveiled enthusiasm.

"I know, Charlie. I heard about your car deal." Burton gripped the handrail and looked his son in the eye. "Look, I need a shower, and I need to eat, and I'd like to talk with your mother. We can go to the dealership tomorrow."

Charlie's face conveyed immediate dismay. "No way, Dad!" Charlie put on his best pleading expression. "I've begged this guy to hold a car for me all day. I promised him we'd be in this evening."

"Think they will run out of Mustang GTs in Southern California anytime soon?"

Charlie's eyes widened. "How'd you know it was a Mustang?"

Burton laughed again. "Because it's all you've talked about for months now! When you took down the *Sports Illustrated* swimsuit posters and replaced them with Mustang posters, that was my first clue."

"It's a *special* car! Only 300 of them were made with this paint job—wait until you see it, Dad. It has everything, and it's a sweet deal. I can give you all the details while we drive down there. We'll be in and out in no time, I promise. It's all set up."

Burton rolled his eyes, but smiled. "You can tell me after I take a shower and eat. Call your Mustang guy and tell him you'll be there later." He saw Charlie slowly absorb the fact that his dream would be delayed another arduous hour. But resilient, Charlie quickly bounded down the stairs and helped Julie prepare dinner. If he couldn't control the process, he could at least expedite it.

Burton took a long shower. He let the hot water ease the knots in his back. After, he shaved and dressed, whistling, thinking about the research he'd need to do for the new airline idea. Feeling like a new man, he headed back downstairs. His stomach growled in anticipation. He knew Julie would be preparing something fabulous.

Charlie popped out of nowhere, blocking Burton's path to the kitchen. "Mom said dinner will be ready in about an hour. So we should run over to the dealership."

"I thought we agreed I could eat, Charlie. I haven't had anything all day."

"Well, dinner isn't ready, so I figured it would be a good time. Hey," he said, delighted with a brain wave, "I've got a Snickers bar here." Like a magician pulling a rabbit out of a hat, Charlie offered a candy bar that looked like it had been at the bottom of his backpack for at least a week.

"Charlie, I've been stuck all week at the Snack Expo. A half-melted and smashed Snickers bar is hardly tempting, nor is it a great negotiation tool. Frankly, I'm surprised at you," Burton teased.

"It'll just take a minute. The sales guy said he may not be able to hold it much longer." Growing more resourceful, Charlie tried another approach. "We could pick up a little something on the way down. Dad, *please*. I kinda promised this guy we'd head over soon."

"Hmmm," smiled Burton, his arms folded. "You sure you're mature enough to drive?"

Charlie shot his father a wounded look. Maturity was his mantra, though he was aware his car quest had been bordering on obsessive. Like any good negotiator, however, he took the comment in stride and doubled back to try again. "I know you're beat, Dad, and I'd hate to get stuck at the dealership later tonight. This guy is ready for us to come in, so it really shouldn't take long. Let me drive you there, and I'll pick something up for you to snack on—my treat—and…," Charlie looked at Burton's softening expression, "…we'll be back for dinner in no time. Then you can *really* relax, because you won't have to go out again."

"OK. Sold." Burton shook Charlie's hand. Julie had watched the whole thing from the kitchen and was simultaneously proud of and exasperated with her son. Burton turned to her and asked, "Where's Sam? She's usually the first to greet me."

Julie stirred something on the stove. "Oh, she's at dance. I doubt she'll be home before you're able to go and come back. She said she'd be home for dinner, though. Megan's mom is dropping her off when it's over." Hands on her hips, she looked at her son and then her husband. "Are you up to this, honey?"

"Do I really have a choice?" Burton poured some coffee into a travel mug. He knew he should feel exhausted after the long day, but truthfully, he was feeling a little energized. He also knew how invested Charlie was in this car thing.

Burton looked forward to settling in later that night with Julie. Charlie would be deep into his new car handbook, and he'd have a chance to talk with her about his idea. "I want to talk when we get home." He kissed her cheek. "I've got a few things I'd like to toss around with you."

"You're not planning another vacation, are you? We haven't been home all that long since the last one."

"Nope, nothing like that." Burton hesitated slightly, then went on. "The new product idea I started telling you about last night."

Julie bit at the corner of her lip but was smiling. "Oh yeah, your airline thing. I forgot." Julie turned back to the stove and adjusted the flame. "I wonder if it's such a good idea. There's already so much going on."

"I've made some notes, and I'd really like to take you through my thinking." She turned back to him, held his gaze for a moment, and then just nodded. Burton glanced at Charlie, who was now literally dancing to get out the door. "Guess we better go before he explodes."

"I'll chill some wine while you're gone. Good luck." She tapped the clean end of her spoon lightly on Burton's chest. "Remember, he got this obsessive streak from you."

Burton grabbed his coffee, and he and Charlie headed out. Under duress, Charlie swung by a local bagel place and watched, wincing as his dad leisurely ordered and asked for a *toasted* bagel, cruelly stretching the delay another 30 seconds. As they finally pulled into the dealership, Charlie waved at a salesman who was chatting idly with another on the front steps.

"Wow, Charlie, they're really busy. Good thing we got here early!" Burton realized Charlie had scarcely heard him; his son was out the door and hurrying up to the sales center.

After a few minutes inside, Burton learned that Charlie had set his sights on a black, two-door Mustang GT convertible with a huge racing stripe running down the side. He had already found out what he needed for insurance, anticipated all safety and mileage questions, looked into the maintenance packages, and prearranged the down payment and financing options. The determined teen had saved money from several summer jobs and had shrewdly built up his own Mustang war chest. Burton saw that his son had managed the transaction with the shrewdness of a seasoned CEO. *Passion can equal experience sometimes*, thought Burton. *Wish I had half the passion that kid does*. He signed his much-coveted signature on the sales agreement and turned to his beaming son. "Congratulations, Charlie. Well done." He thought he saw his son's feet lift off the ground.

Charlie drove home, elated, in his shiny convertible. Burton watched as the car pulled off the lot, top down, the late afternoon sun no rival for Charlie's radiant grin. He had talked non-stop about the countless features of this modern marvel of engineering—and all the friends he'd need to show the car to. As they pulled side by side into the driveway, Charlie leaped out, immediately extolling the exquisite handling and the subtleties of the antilock braking system. Samantha bolted outside and embraced her dad. "Does this mean I get the horse I've always wanted? Megan says she's got room at her place to board it if I want, and now Charlie can take me out there to ride!"

Burton laughed at her quick thinking. "Hold on now. Nice to see you too, honey."

"Of course you know I missed you, Daddy," she said, as though he was being ridiculous. She quickly turned her attention to her brother's new wheels. "Take me somewhere," she squealed to him.

Both were giddy by the time Julie walked down the driveway. "A *convertible*, Charlie? Never once did he mention he was getting a *convertible*, Burton. Is this OK with you?" Julie cast a worried look at her husband.

Burton put his arm around her. "Charlie understands he will need to be careful. From what I saw down at the dealership, our son is organized, focused, and well-informed. And we got a good deal."

"Thanks, Dad. I appreciate your help today." Charlie looked again at his car, grinning from ear to ear. "It's *so* cool."

Burton walked back into the house with Julie, and Charlie

pulled out of the driveway with Samantha for an inaugural drive, honking and waving wildly. Burton sank into the sofa and closed his eyes. Julie handed him a glass of wine and snuggled next to him.

"Honey, are you OK?" Julie looked at Burton with much the same worried expression she had just given Charlie when he drove up in his convertible. "You sounded like you were drowning out there in Chicago, in more ways than one."

Burton sighed. "I was. I am officially sick and tired of that expo. I hated almost every minute of this trip—well, the traveling and the expo for sure." He turned to face her. "I'm really excited about this idea I was trying to tell you about, though. I want to work up this airline thing and see where it goes. I think I'm really on to something. It's got me thinking. Really thinking. It's sad that it's taken so long, but I haven't felt this way in a long time. I want to get into the office early tomorrow and get some research done. I guess I feel like Charlie with his car—eager to get started."

Julie gave Burton a mock-horrified look. "Do *not* act like Charlie! You both will be living in that convertible if you do. I can't take two of you." Then, more serious, she looked him in the eye, studying his face. *She knows this means something to me.* She put her hand on his and said softly, "If you think you want to research something, don't let me stop you."

"Just keep Miss Munchie out of my way. I'm sick of that pixie."

"Now, now. Don't pick on her. She's become part of the family. You are the esteemed mayor of Munchieville, you know." Julie took a sip of wine as she smiled at him. "I know you get sick of all the pink and girly stuff. But it's working. I'd hate to start spinning in a million directions."

"I think I'm really just interested in one direction right now, Julie," Burton said, matter-of-fact. *Does she understand? Can she? Of course she can.* "Remember when you got the idea for the Miss Munchie bar?"

Julie laughed. "I was in the kitchen for weeks. Remember how we had to drive clear to Santa Barbara to find the oat flakes I needed? It was like an ingredient scavenger hunt to find everything. I must have baked a thousand bars in a week."

"I remember coming home from the Goo Bar plant and walking into the house. It smelled wonderful, and you were always excited to have me taste your latest creation."

"That *was* fun," Julie reminisced. Then she looked at Burton, and her eyes drew together with a worried smile. "But honey, why you are bringing all of this up now?"

"I was happy to help you build your dream," Burton ventured. "I loved seeing your energy, your creativity—you had a great vision. It was so easy to get behind your idea, behind *you*."

"You helped make that a reality, every step of the way."

"I was happy to, and I was happy to let go of the Goo Bar to do it. I guess what I am saying is…" Burton paused a moment, looking for the right words. "I've spent a lot of time in Munchieville. I'm ready to follow some of my own dreams for a change."

Burton's tone told her this was more than idle daydreaming. He had always helped clear the path to make things happen. While she had been free to decide where the company went, she had assumed that this was *his* path too, that he was as content as she was. Things were good as far as she was concerned. They had a solid marriage, two healthy and happy children, a comfortable home, freedom to travel at least a couple times a year, and things with the business were good. Munchieville was as close to paradise as they might hope for, she figured. Still, she liked this intensity in her husband. She hadn't seen him so charged up in a long time. But she was a little worried too. Where would this intensity take him? Take *them*? Julie decided not to let it trouble her—for now. She raised her glass and clinked it gently against Burton's. "Here's to you and to Mustang GTs."

Chapter 6

Let's Get Tactical

---

*Strategy is buying a bottle of fine wine
when you take a lady out for dinner.
Tactics is getting her to drink it.*
—Frank Muir

"BURTON!" GAIL SET A STACK of phone messages on Burton's desk. "Nice to see you back. Coffee?"

"Always." Burton looked at his cluttered inbox, grimacing at its sloppy abundance.

"I really shouldn't even ask anymore," Gail said as she handed him his coffee in an oversized mug. "You'll really need it today, though. Fred is fired up to see you. He said it's urgent."

Burton rubbed his eyes slowly. Fred, vice president of operations, was a notorious crank and career handwringer who always had an "urgent matter" to discuss. Fred and Gail had both worked for Burton's father. When the Goo Bar plant closed, Burton had been eager to snap up Fred's operational experience and Gail's administrative precision. That decision, however, had proven bittersweet. Fred's experience had come at a high price—Fred himself.

"It's always 'urgent,' Gail. Do you have any idea what it is this time?"

"The new packaging machine seems to be 'grossly inadequate,'" Gail couldn't hide her smirk, "and rest assured, I have heard *all* about it. I'm quite glad it's your turn."

"Throwin' me under the bus, huh?" Burton took a long draw of coffee and gave Gail a conspiratorial smile.

Without missing a beat, Gail set down a stack of mail and swept out of Burton's office. "Can't blame me, can you?" she said airily and closed the door behind her.

Burton sat quietly for a moment, surveying the chaos on his desk. He knew his airline idea would not survive on the backburner for too long. *Don't get lost. Don't let it get lost.* He looked at his briefcase, thinking of the napkins and notebook inside, beckoning to be reviewed and organized. He punched the intercom and told Gail, "Tell Fred...tell everyone, actually, that I won't be available until this afternoon. I've got a few things I really need to do."

"But you've got a staff meeting in half an hour, Burton. Do you want me to reschedule it?"

Burton winced and looked at his briefcase with a forlorn shrug. *Damn.* With a sigh, he looked at the insistent, blinking red light on his phone, waiting for his reply. "No, no. That's fine, Gail. I forgot about the meeting. See if you can find a block of time for me this afternoon. To quote our buddy, Fred, I've got something urgent I'd like to work on."

As they filed into the conference room, the staff filled the air with their familiar noisy chatter. Fred was the first to sit down. With his usual calculated precision, he scanned the agenda to make sure his equipment issue was top of the list. He nodded at Burton casually as he entered the room, but Burton could see the avid gleam in his eyes and the way his hands tensed over the paper. The nod was just an act. Fred was spoiling for a rant. Burton's father had often called Fred Hacket "Fred Hatchet"—a name that had stuck his entire career. "That crazy son of a bitch," his father had said fondly of Fred. "He cuts through the bull with both arms swingin'." Burton had liked Fred's no-nonsense approach. But over time, he had also begun to realize that Fred didn't just cut the bull, but everything else, too—ideas, enthusiasm, and innovation. He saved his fiercest rancor for Burton; he didn't bother much with those he perceived to be lower in the chain of command. Although Julie had as much authority as Burton, Fred was old school when it came to women in business. He didn't take his issues to her. For better or worse, usually worse, Burton bore the brunt of Fred's negativity and disruption. And, though they shared management level decision-making, Burton and Julie tried to keep their responsibilities and tasks separate as much as possible. This morning, Julie was meeting with the graphic designer who was working on new artwork for the lobby.

"Burton," Fred began, "we've got an urgent issue I'd like to push up on the agenda." The rest of the staff had settled around the table, wisely quiet while Fred launched his opening salvo.

"It's good to be back," Burton said to Gail, unflapped, only half under his breath. Gail, who was taking the meeting minutes, shot Burton her best "I told you so" smirk. Burton turned to the rest of the room. "I understand we have an equipment issue to discuss, and Paul has a cash flow analysis for us." Burton skimmed the agenda. "Looks like we have a lot of odds and ends to address too. So let's get started."

Fred refused to be dismissed so easily. "*Clearly*, the most urgent matter is the new packaging machine. The new system is pure crap. I cannot run an efficient line with that thing. I told—"

"I understand there is an issue, Fred, and we'll get to it." Burton cut him off before he could hit full stride. "Let's start with Paul this morning. I want to make sure we aren't rushed as we review the report."

Fred shot Burton a look of frustration and crossed his arms over his chest. Paul cleared his throat and awkwardly began his presentation. He was a genius with numbers, but a train wreck when it came to reading a room. Just as he always did, Paul went through his report in meticulous detail. Paul was an ideal CFO: he loved accuracy and found beauty in his balance sheets. A man who loved the predictability of numbers, he had exacting standards and a methodical, industrious work ethic that made him a valuable asset to the company. Unfortunately, Paul's presentations had a sleep-inducing quality that soon had the others in the room counting ceiling tiles.

Paul closed his presentation with his sales forecast. Gary Masters, the newly hired vice president of marketing, joined Paul in reviewing the numbers, but he offered a charismatic respite from Paul's dull monotone. In fact, there was something quite gripping about Gary—something Burton hadn't been able to put his finger on yet. Gary was a nationwide-headhunt find. His resume was impressive, his contacts extensive, and from what Burton remembered of his job interview, he was able to quickly assimilate information. Gary had shot back smart, articulate ideas on the spot. In the couple months he'd been at the company, he'd become known for his steady way of getting at things and doing them well. He seemed hard to get to know, perhaps intimidating to some, but he was even-tempered, consistent, and respected throughout the organization. Burton was waiting to see where Gary might be able to help take the company. Now, in the middle of his take on the numbers, Burton found himself wondering how a heavy hitter like Gary might help his airline idea fly. He filed the thought away and dialed back into what Gary was saying. "Unfortunately, our projections on our core products indicate a fairly significant reduction of sales, down almost 13 percent."

"What's the driving factor? What's happening?" Burton asked. He wondered if Julie knew this. They weren't used to downturns, even temporary ones. He wasn't worried about the results, but knew that Julie might react with some alarm. She might not be so supportive of Burton turning his attention to something new if she wanted the company to focus on bolstering what they were already doing instead.

"We've got a delinquency problem caused by delays in shipment; that is a key concern for two of our major distributors," said Paul. "Gary has been getting a lot of heat from those guys." Burton felt himself relax a little. *OK. This can be fixed easily enough.*

"See!" Fred nearly shouted. "Operation difficulties are impacting sales. We've got to deal with it. I *wonder* what could be slowing down the line. Wait. I know… Could it be that packaging machine that doesn't work?" Fred looked triumphant after delivering his bad news.

"Looks like this is a good time to get into your issue, Fred," said Burton. "The floor is yours. What's the problem?"

"Aside from being routinely ignored…," Fred began.

"Aside from that, yes. Let's get into specifics here, Fred." Burton realized he was tapping his foot and stopped.

"You decided to buy this fancy new contraption rather than

simply replace the old machine as I requested. I now have a touchy machine that breaks down frequently and needs lots of special attention." *Touchy, breaks down frequently, needs special attention... Boy, does that sound familiar,* thought Burton as he looked at Fred. He tried not to smile and focused back in on the problem.

"Are you still using the old plastic sheeting? I know the technician I spoke to when we got the machine said it was important to use the new supply."

"Well, I'll switch when we are out of the old stuff. There isn't much difference, and I am not about to waste perfectly good materials because some 20-year-old hotshot wants a nice commission on extras. We paid enough for that thing on its own. It shouldn't need special and expensive materials too."

"It sure does if that's the factor that's derailing production. It does a better job in less time than the old system. I don't care about old plastic sheeting when time is money. If we need to change a few things, let's change them. Why are we messing around? Let's order what we need to get the best result. Are you following the manufacturer's feed rates?" Burton pushed back from the conference table, exasperated.

Fred looked as irritated as Burton felt. He didn't like being challenged like this in front of everyone else. Burton preferred to address individual performance breakdowns one on one, but Fred had harassed too many other departments when he was dropping the ball in areas himself. Fred started, faltering, "You don't understand…"

"No, Fred. *You* don't understand. We are not going back to the old system. The new design meets federal standards better, and it produces a cleaner, more attractive package. It is well reviewed and reliable—*if* used correctly."

"Those guidelines the manufacturer puts out are like speed limits. No one actually follows them. I don't have time to follow them and meet production goals too."

"But we aren't meeting production goals, Fred. I think that's Burton's point," Gary said coolly, but with authority. Burton was surprised by his forthrightness, as the newcomer on the team, but he appreciated the backup. He wasn't the only one who saw Fred's unwavering commitment to interference. "With all due respect Fred, from what I've seen, this is an *extremely* predictable company. Not much changes around here. One small equipment change shouldn't be that overwhelming. This isn't a big deal, is it? So we need to order a different weight of plastic sheeting. Let's keep our perspective."

Burton could see that Fred was rankled, but he remained silent. Gary turned to Burton and caught his eye, almost but not quite smiling. *Was that a show of support, or posturing?* Burton found himself wondering. But mostly, he was halted by Gary's words, "This is an extremely predictable company. Not much changes around here." *So, he sees it, too—after only a few weeks. We're that predictable. We're that...boring. I've gotten that boring.*

The meeting continued. Fred had retreated to his corner, and, mercifully, he kept quiet as the rest of the group clipped through the agenda. Burton heard himself murmuring "sure" and "sounds good," but his attention was only half there. *Not much changes around here. It is extremely predictable...* Gary Masters, the sharp heavy hitter, was on to them already. And he had just made the same speech to Fred that Burton had once delivered to his father at the Goo Bar factory—pleading with the old guard to roll with a few minor changes. *Just sell them bars, boy. Just sell them bars.*

"Burton?" Paul said, snapping him out of his thoughts.

Burton glanced around the table, his staff polite but anxious to get out of the meeting. "There's one more thing," he began. *What are you doing?* he thought. *Are you ready for this? Are they ready for this?* Burton felt his heart begin to pound. *I don't care anymore. I'm rocking the boat.* "I've been thinking seriously about something…considering a new initiative for us at Hall's. Something outside the Miss Munchie line." Out of the corner of his eye, he saw Gary lean forward in his chair. Burton continued, "I was thinking of developing an airline division, of working up a new product line specifically for airline distribution."

"Huh?" Fred said, almost mocking. "What are you smoking, Burton? You've never said anything about this." The staff looked at Burton, bewildered but now fully awake. Fred stood up and gathered his notes. "You folks go ahead and discuss whatever this is. I've got work to do."

"You want to sell Miss Munchie bars to the airlines?" Paul asked after Fred had swept out of the room. Leave it to Paul to be logical, linear. *Who can blame him, working in this place?*

Burton stood up and began to walk slowly around the table. "No, we need to design something entirely new. I met Susan Jenson, a vice president over at Brigham Air, while I was at the Snack Expo. I met her quite by accident, actually. She asked me if I had an antacid," he grinned. The staff chuckled knowingly. "We got talking, and she told me how Brigham has been searching for a hearty, single-serving snack food for their in-flight service. She also said she hasn't found anything suitable out there. Brigham is prepared to dish out $14 million annually for the right product line, and they're willing to share in product development. That really got me thinking."

"So how do the Miss Munchie bars fit in?" asked Gary.

"They don't. Like I said, we need to work up something entirely new. It may have some similar ingredients—maybe not.

I've begun the research." An awkward silence filled the room as the staff digested what Burton was saying.

"We don't have any experience in the airline industry," said Paul.

"I know, but we do have experience with wholesome convenience foods. I think we could be a good fit for Brigham. And, as Gary has pointed out, it may not hurt to shake things up a little around here. I've made some notes on strategy. I'm going to get them organized, and I have the name and number of an airline consultant so we can discuss the possibility. I recognize this is mostly speculative right now, but I thought you should know there may be some significant changes ahead." Burton slowly returned to his seat and sat down. He folded his hands and rested them on the table. All eyes were on Burton. Finally, Gary broke the silence.

"Good thing Fred left the room," he laughed. "The new packaging machines have nearly killed him. A new product will really send him spinning."

"I'm not too worried about Fred. I won't have time for any antics, but we'll need to keep up cash flow to get this going. We need to get the line running and crank out bars. I know Fred can do that once we get past the packaging machine drama."

"Well," said Paul slowly, "we'll really need to work out the funding. I need some idea of the incremental spending, and we'll need some time to figure out just what we can afford to spend on this. A promise from Brigham to help with product development is one thing, but we'd have to have something ready to pitch to get that commitment. That'll take some dedicated human and financial resources."

"I've already been working that up, Paul. We may need to be a little more flexible in the beginning. You're going to have to hang in there until I have a better picture of what we're working with."

"You've never mentioned any of this, Burton," said Gary. "I like the idea, but I have to say I really wasn't expecting it."

"This will be a change for all of us. It isn't a typical move for this company; we haven't had a new strategy in a long time. This market is definitely worth a serious look. I think it's time, too." He could see he had to win over the skeptics somehow. They needed to know the *why* behind his decision to move forward.

"The forecasted decline has been chalked up to production problems," Burton said, looking around the conference table, "but we've not discussed the lack of growth. We have been stagnant, and sales haven't increased for many quarters. I know the health bar market has a lot more players than it did 15 years ago. I'd like us to pull our heads out of the sand long enough to look around and see what we can do *in addition* to making Miss Munchie bars." He saw a few tentative nods. He also saw a couple people check their watches. "OK. That's good for now. Thanks for your time and attention. Now I'm sure we've all got a lot to do." With that, the meeting was adjourned.

Burton sat and watched the room begin to clear. Gail patted his shoulder supportively as she passed by. Gary took his time gathering his things. When he could see that everyone was gone, he got up and sat in the seat next to Burton's.

"What you're talking about sounds exciting. I know I'm always up for a challenge," Gary said, grinning. Burton was glad to finally hear some wholehearted enthusiasm about his idea. He knew Gary had seen a lot of ventures gather steam and succeed— and he'd probably helped get them there. Gary kept on, "I know I've only just started here, but if you want any help with this, let me know. In fact," he paused and looked over Burton's shoulder, considering something, "I could use some of my contacts in the marketing network to get a read on what air travelers are looking for. It sounds like you've got the airline's perspective covered with your consulting contact, but it might be good to scope out what customers want. You know, the man on the ground, so to speak." He laughed and leaned back in his chair.

Burton liked Gary's initiative and strategic thinking. "That sounds like a great idea. I'll get a better sense of how we might approach our research after I talk to Mike Collier, the consultant. Why don't you cook on some of those ideas in the meantime?" He extended his hand to shake Gary's. "Thanks for your positive attitude and commitment to make things work well around here. We're lucky to have you."

"I'm very happy to be here," Gary replied. "And I'm always on the right side of a good idea." *How great would it be to have an ally, someone who's really on my side?* Burton mused. He felt himself relax at the thought of not having to go this alone. Some of the rest of the staff might be reluctant to try something new. Fred would definitely drag his feet. But Gary—he was eager to get started, to be part of some adventure. Burton knew it would definitely be an adventure.

Back in his office, he sifted through his sundry pile of notes until he found the number Morty had given him for Mike Collier. A little knot of anticipation mixed with some anxiety developed in his stomach as he dialed the number. *Here we go. Let the adventure begin.*

Chapter 7

Validation

> You're dealing with the demon of external validation. You can't beat external validation. You want to know why? Because it feels sooo good.
> —Barbara Hall

BURTON SAT AT A QUIET TABLE in the restaurant, waiting for Mike Collier to arrive. They'd had a brief but already-informative conversation a few days earlier. Burton had shared how he'd gotten Mike's card from Morty and what he was hoping to achieve in a product for airlines. The two men had talked easily. Burton liked Mike right away. He gave feedback on Burton's idea on the spot, as though consulting was natural to him, something he did just for fun. He seemed forthright and trustworthy, which Burton needed at this stage; Mike had offered right at the start to sign a confidentiality agreement, something Burton hadn't even considered. Burton had to twist Mike's arm just to convince him to accept a free dinner in exchange for his advice.

In the half hour they spoke on the phone, Burton learned that all the airlines were struggling to create some kind of competitive advantage and that food might be a promising angle. The two men joked about the fact that bad airline food had almost become a brand in itself. But Mike had warned, "You're not alone. There are several companies trying to work their way into the airline market and a few major players that have been there for years."

"I understand," Burton had said thoughtfully. He knew already that Mike would be a tremendous resource. They had arranged to have dinner the following Monday evening.

Monday was finally here, and Burton was eagerly looking forward to this meeting. Just before seven o'clock, a tall but slight man walked into the restaurant and paused, scanning the room. *It must be Mike*, thought Burton. He raised his hand when the man looked again in his direction. Sure enough, Burton's wave was met with a smile and a look of slight relief. Mike approached the table. "Burton Hall?" he said, extending his hand. "You're early."

"I'm glad you could meet with me, Mike. I wouldn't miss it." Burton motioned for Mike to have a seat. "I also love this restaurant," Burton admitted. Mike had suggested the spot, since it was close to his office. It was a quiet, ranch-style steakhouse. "My wife is not a fan of red meat or gravy the way I am. She's vegan and something of a nutritional crusader. I've got to tell you—I'm happy to not be at the House of Tofu and Veggies for a change."

"I feel your pain," laughed Mike. "My wife is a low-carb maniac. The kids and I have resorted to sneaking bagels into the house when she's asleep."

The two men chatted easily. The conversation was casual and friendly until they had both ordered. "Now that we've ordered our steak and potatoes," Burton grinned, "let's get down to business." He began to tell Mike the story behind his idea. Mike listened closely and soon was filling in gaps for Burton about the mechanics of airline food service. Burton hadn't realized that packaging was such a pivotal issue. Soon he and Mike were brainstorming ideas to address labeling and storage issues. Burton was scribbling his thoughts on cocktail napkins, a now-familiar medium.

"You're really on to something, Burton. I like your thinking," Mike affirmed.

"You've helped me immensely, Mike. This really focuses things. I wanted some validation from someone within the industry to make sure I was on the right track." Burton shifted gears slightly. "Tell me, if you don't mind, a little about passenger expectations."

"People are definitely more health conscious. They don't want something greasy or salty when they have to be inactive for several hours on a flight. Of course, there are a million different special diets and concerns; people love finding things that fit their personal preferences. They also have a lot of time to sit and think about what they're being served—plenty of time to complain if they're disappointed, and with a captive audience. There has been a lot of good market research that's been done recently. It's a lot to go over."

"Funny you should mention that," Burton said, smiling at how things seemed to be falling into place. "I recently hired a new marketing vice president, and he's eager to help with this project. I guess he's got some old contacts who can put him in touch with good market research on this."

"Well, then you're halfway there," Mike said. "That's great." He continued, "There is a real need and a gap in the current service. I know that you're looking at a real opportunity, Burton.

You look like you're enjoying yourself, too. It's nice to see someone with energy and ideas."

"I really am enjoying myself," Burton nodded. "My gut tells me I'm on to something."

"Just don't tell your wife what *is* actually in your gut. I don't want the vegans coming after me." Mike and Burton laughed heartily.

"Make sure you don't come home with any breadcrumbs on your tie either. The carb police can be tough too."

"Tell me about it," Mike said. "Well, good luck, Burton. Let me know if you've got any other questions, and keep me posted. I'd like to see what Hall's comes up with."

Me too, Burton thought. They had been at the restaurant for three and a half hours, but the time had flown by. On his way to the parking lot, Burton called Julie to say he was on his way home. Then he dialed Gary's office line and left a voicemail message: "Gary. It's Burton. I just had a great dinner meeting with the airline consultant. Looks like we're on to something. I'd like you to connect with the marketing contacts you mentioned the other day to see what data they can give us on the consumer side. Let's keep in touch." He turned the car engine over. It roared to life and then settled into a low, steady hum.

Burton got home and walked into the kitchen to find Julie cleaning up the last of the dishes. "Hey there, how'd *your* dinner go?" he said, kissing her lightly on the cheek.

"Charlie brought a friend for dinner, but neither of them was too excited about my lentil loaf."

"Gee, I'm sorry I missed it," Burton said facetiously.

"I'm sure you are." Julie gave Burton a semi-scowl. "I can smell the prime rib on your breath. Traitor."

Burton laughed, "You may not believe this, but they didn't

have lentil loaf on the menu. I had to improvise. A guy does the best he can, you know."

Julie rolled her eyes and threw a dishtowel at him. "I know. You can help me dry, Mr. Omnivore. How did your dinner go, aside from the shocking lack of lentils?"

"It went well. I'm really glad I met with Mike. He has a lot of insight and knows the industry. I got some great feedback on my idea, and he answered many of my questions. It would have taken me months to research what we went over, and I can't believe it only cost me a dinner. Great guy."

"Good. I'm glad." Julie leaned against the counter, facing him with her arms folded. "I chatted a bit with Gail yesterday. She said you pitched this whole thing to the staff at the meeting. She said it seemed to be a bit of a surprise. I guess I'm a little surprised too. I knew you were chewing on some ideas, but I didn't know you were ready to go to the staff with them. You're serious about this, aren't you."

Burton dried the pan he was holding. "Yes, I am. I'm excited about it too," he said without looking up.

Julie pressed on. "Well, I've been thinking about this airline angle too. Are you sure it's a good idea? It seems like such a drastic move. Do we need a big change?"

Burton slid the pan back into the cupboard and dried his hands slowly as he looked at Julie. "You look like you're worried."

"I am," she sighed. "I honestly wonder if this is a good idea. The kids are getting older, and we finally have time to do more, to get out and travel, to spend time together. I'm surprised you want to start something new right now. We've been lucky, right? We have so much. Maybe we don't need to start scrambling again."

"I know what you're saying. I do." Burton hung up the towel

and turned to his wife. "That's part of the reason I haven't been willing to rock the boat before now. It's been easy to just flow with the current. But it's almost gotten *too* easy, or... I don't know...boring."

"Why haven't you said anything about this before? You've seemed happy. I know *I've* been happy." She almost looked hurt.

"The business has always been about bringing *your* vision to life. I think you've created a wonderful product, built on a great idea and all the things you really believe in. I've enjoyed watching you fulfill your dream, and I love the success we've had. I just really need to work on this—to see my own vision become a reality, the way yours has."

"But this is *our* company, Burton. It started as my idea, but you're the brains and brawn of Munchieville. You're one of the biggest reasons all this has been successful." She sat down at the breakfast bar. "I just don't know where this is coming from, you know. I think I'm beginning to understand, but it seems like taking a big risk when we're not being forced to and when we've got so much more to lose."

"I don't want to take anything away from the company and what we've done with it—together. I just need to do this, to at least try. 'Business as usual' feels more and more stifling to me—and the things that keep happening, the way things seem to be unfolding around me are... It's amazing, really. It's only been a few days, and I feel like I've already covered so much ground."

Julie looked out the window at the lights from the valley. "I know the world of Miss Munchie has always been my thing—I do. You've always been a good sport about the logo and image and everything, even when pink isn't your best color," she smiled. Then the smile disappeared from her face again. "I just worry, Burton. Is this the right time? Is it worth the risk? We've been so lucky. It seems a little wrong to ask for more."

Burton thought about his wife's words. She'd given voice to some of the thoughts he'd had in the back of his mind, nagging at him from time to time. He had a healthy, happy family and a beautiful home. They had security as well as luxury, and that was so much. Was it selfish, even greedy, to chase his own dream now, when so many other dreams were already right in front of him? *I can't shake this need to try, though.* "It feels right, Julie. I feel like I need this. I haven't felt this engaged in something in a long time. It's not about seeking more. It's *doing* more, seeing the end product take shape. Do you remember when the first box of Miss Munchie bars came off the line—remember how that made you feel?"

"Yes," she answered softly.

Burton sat beside her at the breakfast bar. She leaned her head on his shoulder. "Julie," he said, "this isn't about growing the business—not in terms of numbers anyway. But it is about growth, about pushing myself, and maybe even the staff, to stretch and explore and enjoy what we *do*—more than we enjoy the lifestyle it gives us."

Julie slid her arm around his waist. "I can see you're all fired up again. I haven't seen this Burton in a long time, the one I started the business with. I *do* like seeing you so energetic, so… happy."

Burton pulled back so he could look her in the eyes. "So, you're OK with this?"

Julie took a long breath, as if she was still answering the question for herself. She looked at Burton, at the almost childlike gleam in his eye. She didn't want to rob him of that delight.

"Yes, I think I am, as long as we don't cancel vacations and family time. I think my biggest worry is about losing that. Those early days in Munchieville were pretty tough. I'm not sure I ever want to go back there."

"What's great is now we have a whole lot more experience and resources. We're not on that steep learning curve anymore. All those years behind us can work *for* us now."

"I know you're right," Julie smiled.

Burton was beaming, happy to have his wife's understanding and her blessing. "Just one thing though, honey," he chided. "I am keeping both you and Miss Munchie out of the loop. I think you'll both understand."

"What? You're not going to let me at least choose your product's color scheme?"

"Not a chance, sweetie," he said, kissing the top of her head as he got up. "I want to see if the kids are asleep." He left the room.

Julie called after him, "I do have some favorite shades of blue, you know!" She smiled to herself, then rested her chin in her hands, biting her lower lip.

Chapter 8

Strategy by the Numbers

> Action on the move creates its own route;
> creates to a very great extent
> the conditions under which is it to be fulfilled,
> and thus baffles all calculation.
> —Henri Bergson

THE NEXT MORNING, Burton met with Paul to once again review the financials and look for ways to fund product development. "I do think this is viable, Burton. Based on some of the figures you and Gary have given me, I think there may be a real opportunity here. If we can get Brigham Air to jointly fund the development phase, so much the better. In fact, from a numbers perspective, we'd need their backing to move forward with this. And we still need an actual product and a hell of a lot more cash."

"I know. We need to put a solid plan together, but I think we're close. We'll get together with Gary and start getting a lot more specific. I don't think we have any issues we can't figure out. I think we've got all the data we need now." Burton poured a large cup of coffee and motioned to Paul. "Coffee?"

"No, thanks. I had some in Gary's office. No wonder you like him. He's as addicted as you are. He's also pretty fired up about your plan. He's asked me a million questions. I think you struck a chord with him."

"Good," Burton said once he had swallowed a couple gulps of coffee. "We'll answer some of the big questions, for Gary and everyone else, at the staff meeting tomorrow. It's time to give people a better idea of where we're going."

"I'll put together a PowerPoint for tomorrow."

"Think brief, Paul. You tend to go a little crazy."

"I'll keep it under three hours," Paul joked. "I know how much you love detailed financial analysis."

Burton rolled his eyes. "That's me! Let's keep it simple. We'll look at the projected start-up costs. You can focus on highlighting the major projections, and I'll handle *why* we're doing all this in the first place."

Burton went back to his office and sat down. Ceremonially, he pulled out his diary and motley stack of notes—every scribble he'd marked down so far. *This is my dream, in a pile of paper. All right here. Something that's really mine.* He opened his diary to the page where he had originally tossed around ideas for the airlines. He made a note to refer to today's date. Jumping ahead a few pages to where his writing stopped, he began to record the highlights and key findings from his journey so far. He recorded data, bits of information he'd gathered from Mike Collier and Gary's market research, and, most rewarding of all, his recent mental state. He wrote about the new energy and vitality he was experiencing, his sense of coming alive in ways he hadn't felt in years, and his vision for the hopefully not-too-distant future—when he'd be on a flight to the next snack expo, thanking the flight attendant for a delicious, satisfying, and wholesome snack, Hall's first product launch in years. He didn't write it down, but Burton also imagined the conversation he'd have with George; he'd be the one with news—real news—to share for a change. Burton laughed at himself, this impulse to prove himself to a colleague. That would be gravy. What really mattered was that he was following a dream—his dream—through to the end.

Burton scooped the pile of precious papers back into his drawer. He laid his diary on top, last of all. Tomorrow at the staff meeting, he'd rally his troops for the next push in making his dream a reality.

The next afternoon, Burton and his staff met again as a group. With confidence, he laid out the action plan for the next several months, underlining the reasons this new venture was so important. Burton sensed that his staff, for the most part, were capturing the vision of a more vital, energetic workplace where change was possible and maybe even welcomed. This time, he sensed more buy-in, even semi-enthusiastic support. Fred, of course, was a naysayer through and through. But Burton was amused at the way most of the staff now saw aligning with the initiative as an opportunity to get under Fred's skin. Fred had few friends in the company.

"So after looking at the numbers, I'd like to begin in earnest and get some product development going right away. I think this is a great opportunity, and I'm looking forward to getting started." Burton released his staff.

Once again, Gary lingered. "You know, Burton. I'd love to

get more involved with this project somehow. I really believe in it. Are you looking for someone to take the lead on this?" Gary asked carefully.

"Wow." Burton looked at his vice president of marketing with surprise. "I guess I've only ever thought of this as a team play. We know what success will look like. Now we need a plan to get there. I think it's going to take all our human resources to achieve."

"I agree entirely." Gary flipped through his copy of Paul's presentation. "I also think you probably need someone to run point on this, to make sure all of those resources come together. I know how busy you are with what we've already got on the go. Just a thought, but I'd love to have the chance to really make this fly."

Burton studied Gary's face. He had energy Burton rarely saw. Gary was the husband of one of Julie's closest friends, and she had been eager to see him join the company. Of course, from a business perspective, Burton had been impressed with Gary's solid resume. So far, he'd been hardworking, more than competent, and easy to work with. Despite that, Burton had felt a kind of bored reservation in Gary. *Maybe he's just like you.* He had never seemed all that engaged or excited—until talk of the airline project began. Maybe Gary would be an even stronger player if Burton could involve him fully in something he was eager to do. *Perhaps I do need to delegate some of this. Then I can focus on the larger picture. Julie will worry less about how I'm spending my time if I hand off some of the work.* "Well, I do have a company to run," laughed Burton, "and we all know how behind I am in performance reviews. I'm happy and flattered you're as interested as you are. So I guess I'm asking you to be champion of the new initiative."

"That's great!" Gary exclaimed, pumping Burton's hand. "I've been looking for something like this, Burton. I've always wanted to create a product from the ground up."

"Well, we're definitely at ground level with this," Burton said with a sigh. "But I think the sky's the limit, too."

After Gary strode out, Burton stayed in the conference room to write down some thoughts that had occurred to him during his presentation. The table was a chaotic mess of paper, charts, and coffee cups. *Evidence of a busy workplace. It's beautiful.* Burton had given everyone a clear sense of purpose and direction on the project, and he'd issued the first round of tasks to accomplish his plan. He felt like he was really moving now, and his staff seemed to be moving with him. He loved the new charge of energy he sensed in the office.

He knew there was also some fear. Undoubtedly, his staff worried about the changes ahead. Change, moving out into the unknown, was always hard. Burton knew his best weapon to fight that fear was a clear plan. *Do I know where I'm going? Can I ask people to take a leap with me? What if I'm wrong?* His thoughts were swimming again. Gail came into the conference room and surveyed the debris. "How can a handful of adults create such a mess?"

Burton chuckled, "Yeah, it looks like a bomb exploded in here, but it was a great meeting, Gail. We got a lot accomplished."

"I almost wish I had been able to sit in on this one. It sounded like you were having a good time in here. I kept hearing you and Gary laughing."

"We were. Gary has really stepped up on the project. I think I'll have him supervise product development. He seems to have his finger on the pulse of what consumers want, and he's motivated. It's almost too good to be true, you know. I'm surprised he's so eager. The rest of the staff seem a lot more...cautiously optimistic. But maybe he's used to a more dynamic workplace where he came from. He seemed happy to hear about a change in the routine."

"It sounds like he really understands what you're trying to achieve," she said as she began picking cups off the table.

Burton stood and began helping Gail clean up, stretching his legs after the long meeting. "I hope so," he said. "I know I'll need some help if I'm going to pull this off."

"What's on your agenda for this afternoon?" Gail asked as they headed out of the conference room.

"I'm beat, Gail. I think I'm going to get home early, take Willard for a long walk, and have a nice dinner with Julie and the kids. My son has been missing in action since he got his new car. Julie's threatened to take his keys unless he eats dinner with us tonight."

"You know, you don't have anything scheduled for tomorrow..." Gail conspired.

"Hmmm." Burton welcomed the possibility of spending some time at home. "I may just work at home tomorrow then. Everyone has plenty to do here. They might even appreciate it if I stayed out of their way for a bit. Maybe I'll go to the airport."

"The airport? Tell me you're not running away!"

"No, don't worry. Not yet, anyway. I want to watch how the food is loaded onto the planes. That's one real-world piece we're still missing. I'd like to see just how they take normal food and manage to crush it, make it stale and soggy, and then suck all the flavor out just before the flight."

Gail laughed. "Exactly! Figure out how they engineer those bags of pretzels too. They're all but impossible to open."

"And isn't it clever how they get them to explode all over the place when they finally do open?" added Burton. "Hey, where's the company video camera? I think I'll get some footage while I'm at the airport so I can share it with the team."

Gail stopped in the middle of the hallway. "Burton, they're not going to let you watch the planes being loaded, and if you try to videotape the process, you'll probably get hauled away by anti-terrorism agents. You *might* be able to arrange something if you use the right channels, but you can't just show up tomorrow and hang out with a camera. They'll think you're Osama bin Burton!"

Burton sighed. "You're right. I don't mean to cause an international incident here. Damn. I really wanted to check out the meal services."

"I do have an idea. I doubt you'll like it much, but it's a possibility, and it'll get you what you're after."

"What's that?"

"You just leave it to me, Burton. And I'll be expecting a juicy little raise—after you finally complete my performance evaluation." She already had the phone in her hand and was waving him to the elevator. She mouthed, "I'll call you. Get out of here."

He was glad she was looking after this for him. It was one less item on his already-full mental plate.

Chapter 9

The Field Trip

We all learn by experience, but some of us
have to go to summer school.
—Peter De Vries

THE FOLLOWING MORNING, Burton found himself at the airport's main terminal, surrounded by at least 30 preschoolers. It turned out that Gail's five-year-old grandson had recently been on an airport tour with his class. He'd told Gran all about it, including how big "moving black carpets" carried luggage into the airplane, and about the "shiny metal boxes" that the "big machines" loaded onto the plane. Gail assumed from her own experience flying that the metal boxes carried the food. She'd tracked down the person at the airport who arranged the school tours and sweet-talked him into letting Burton tag along on one. He was lined up as a volunteer helper.

When Gail had called him the night before, Burton could tell she was up to something. She had explained what she'd done, pointing out how it was perfect. He would have access to everything he wanted to see, and he wouldn't have to worry about sight lines, surrounded by knee-high kids. "Now, you enjoy preschool tomorrow, and be a good boy. Make sure you hold hands, and don't touch anything," she had giggled.

"Very funny, Gail. But thank you. This will help." He had to admit, the idea was brilliant.

Burton knew Gail was enjoying the thought of her boss hanging around with the kids all day. Julie also took full advantage of the silliness of the situation. She packed him a lunch in one of Sam's old lunchboxes and handed him a gold star sticker for brushing his teeth. *This better be worth it.* He knew it would be time well spent trying to understand the business, but he was willing to bet money that a day in preschool was going to be noisy—and probably sticky too. And if Fred ever got wind of it, he'd never let Burton live it down.

Once he'd arrived, it was easy to spot his group. The kids were in a meandering line near a ticket agent, excitedly putting on their name tags. Burton walked up and introduced himself to the airport tour guide and the teachers. They greeted him warmly, and soon he was decked out with a name tag of his own and an undersized captain's hat. "This is quite a challenge, Mr. Hall. You'll soon see." The teacher took charge and gave marching orders: "Adults at the head of the line and at the back. Don't allow anyone to stray. And if you can, try to prevent them from touching *anything*."

Burton looked down and saw a young boy in a red sweater who had grabbed his hand, his sweaty, small fingers clutching Burton's in what amounted to a pint-sized death grip.

"That's Jeremy," the teacher informed Burton, as if that would explain everything.

Burton looked down at the boy, remembering how Charlie

had looked at that age. "Nice to meet you, Jeremy. I'm Mr. Hall."

Jeremy gave Burton a shy nod, and the two followed the rest of the class as the airport adventure began. Burton saw that this was not going to be a leisurely stroll through the airport. It was a huge undertaking to get all the children to move in the same direction. Five minutes into the trip, Burton had nearly forgotten he was in an airport, let alone needing to critically analyze operations, but he had to admit it was kind of fun, and Jeremy still needed somebody's hand to hold, after all.

The children watched with wide-eyed wonderment as the baggage conveyers snaked through the loading bay. It was a whirl of activity and noise, and the children dutifully followed their teachers and listened to the tour guide; they were intimidated by the machinery. The children peppered the adults with questions, many of which were about what happens if someone needs to go to the bathroom while they're on the airplane. The tour guides were nonplussed about "poop" at 30,000 feet, and Burton was impressed with their ability to answer the questions with such tact. Burton whispered into Jeremy's ear, "Hey, Jeremy, ask them what 'blue ice' is. I've always wondered about that." With a giggle, Jeremy smiled and raised his hand and waved it wildly to try to get the guide's attention.

They finally reached the area where crews were loading food and beverages. After just a few moments, it became clear that this was a chaotic operation. Burton could see there was a need to impose some order down here. Carts, bags, and cola bottles seemed to be stacked everywhere. Some of the food was in direct sunlight, without refrigeration. Burton thought about all the ways simple packaging could improve the system, matching the food with specific flight routes and standardizing carton sizes. He could see that creating better food safety labels would also help immensely. He asked the tour guide if he could videotape the procedure using his cell phone.

"Don't let me see you do it, man. Be cool, and be quick, OK? You aren't supposed to tape in here."

Burton asked Jeremy if he would mind letting go of his hand, just for a minute, so he could take a picture. Jeremy looked a bit miffed at the suggestion; clearly, releasing Burton's hand was not on his agenda. Suddenly, Jeremy's face lit up. He let go of Burton's hand and smiled, "OK, ready. Take my movie!"

Burton was puzzled, and then it dawned on him. Jeremy thought Burton was taking his picture. The little boy was waiting, straight as a soldier with a lopsided grin, for Burton to capture his airport adventure. Burton saw the eager looks of 30-some other little people, all waiting to be in the movie. He obliged them and, after asking the group to move just a nudge to the left, he was able to tape the loading operation as well as Ms. Garcia's preschool class. And he made sure Jeremy was in every frame.

After the tour, Burton sat in a coffee shop at the airport, writing his ideas down before he could forget them, his mind whirling with new possibilities. He was eager to report his findings and to brainstorm with Gary and the rest of his team. As he scribbled his notes, he was careful to protect the small certificate he had laid on the table in front of him. It read, "I was a good boy at Los Angeles International Airport." That, Burton knew, was going to go up on the refrigerator just as soon as he got home.

Chapter 10

Below the Belt

We laugh at honor and are shocked
to find traitors in our midst.
—C. S. Lewis

AFTER HIS FIELD TRIP, Burton went back to the office to work on strategy with his team. His excitement was catching. All the key office players put their all into coming up with the best development plan possible. Even Fred, with his perpetually sour disposition, helped by finding all the flaws or shortsighted plans that would have caught them off guard at later stages. *That guy can come in handy after all*, Burton figured. Gary was sharp—a great contributor. He'd really done his marketing homework. By the end of a three-day strategic planning retreat off-site, they had a full product development plan, cost and revenue projections, lines on suppliers, storage and shipping criteria, and an elaborate branding and marketing plan—all laid out in graphs, charts, and spreadsheets, thanks to Paul's keen attention to detail. Burton was thrilled to see it all coming together. *See Dad*, he thought, *life is bigger than Goo Bars. Your son's dreams are much bigger.*

He gave the team the next day off, creating an extended weekend as a reward.

The following Monday, Burton got a late-afternoon call from Mike Collier. "Mike! It's nice to hear from you. How've you been?"

"Really good, Burton. Listen, I've got a question for you. You have a Gary Masters working for you, right?"

"I do. He's working with me on the airline project right now. He's really backing the project. Why do you ask?"

There was a long pause before Mike spoke again. "He's got about four calls in to me. I was wondering if you wanted me to deal directly with Gary. I have to say I was sort of expecting to continue working with you."

"He has calls in to you?" Burton asked, somewhat alarmed. *That's strange. What's going on? What am I missing here?*

"His messages indicate that he wants to meet. As you know, I have limited time right now. I'd really prefer to keep this simple."

"I understand. I wanted to talk to you about your time, by the way. You need to send me an invoice. I owe you a whole lot more than what that dinner covered."

Mike laughed. "Let's discuss that farther down the road. I don't think you can afford me just yet. I would appreciate working with just you, though."

"I agree. I'll talk to Gary and call him off. He's a bit overzealous, I'm afraid."

"Not a problem. I just thought you should know. How are things coming along? Are you ready to send samples to the tasting committee?"

"I don't know much about that process yet. How important is the group to sales?"

"The major airlines always run tasting committees. They run everything through them, and I mean everything—coffee, toast, even bottled water. They're a professional board and have some pretty exacting standards. They've got a multipoint rating system. The feedback really can make or break you. Anything you develop needs to sail through with flying colors."

"Or you don't fly, huh."

"Nope. You're grounded," said Mike. "They run the panels twice a year. I think the next one is in about a month. If you want to get a contract for next year, you'll need to be ready."

"Wow. OK, we need to get moving. Our test kitchen is presenting some samples to the team right away here. Looks like the timing of your advice couldn't be any better." He looked at his watch and realized the samples meeting had already started.

"Miss the next round and you won't get another chance for six months."

"I appreciate this, Mike. I'm glad we talked."

"You get a green light from this group, and you can expect purchase orders—a lot of them."

After he hung up, Burton sat quietly at his desk for a moment, puzzled. He was surprised Gary had contacted Mike without discussing it with him first. He didn't want to squelch his enthusiasm, but he wondered if Gary was a bit of a loose cannon, going ahead without being careful. Burton decided he'd talk to Gary when he saw him at the product sampling. Perplexed, but eager to see what the food engineers had come up with, he headed for the boardroom.

Burton walked into the room where the production and food engineering teams had already gathered. Gary was missing. Burton was greeted by Robert Maxim, also known as Maximum Bob, in his usual booming voice. "Hey there, Mr. Hall!"

"Good morning, Bob. I'm excited to see what you have for us today." Burton had been told the quirky food-preparation supervisor had spent hours in the test kitchen brainstorming ideas. Bob was a tall, hulking man with a mass of curly red hair, which was usually at least partially tamed by a hairnet. He'd worked for Hall's for years now. No one could quite remember how he had managed to get through the job interview, but somehow, despite his oversize black glasses, red tennis shoes, and awkward appearance, he had become one of the company's most beloved characters. He was also incredibly talented in the kitchen. Even though he looked more like a Spam and Top Ramen kind of guy, Bob had a gourmet's palate and high standards for all the ingredients used on the production line and especially for the results.

"Let's see what you've come up with," said Burton, gesturing toward the bars carefully aligned on the table.

"Sure thing, Mr. Hall," said Bob. The windows in the conference room rattled a little when he spoke, leaving no doubt as to how he had earned his nickname. "We have five samples here. We've thought a lot about the taste and texture of each bar while trying to work up something a little more filling than our Miss Munchie bars. But we've also worked at keeping overall fat and sugar content as low as possible."

Debbie Fritz, a production manager on the team, looked puzzled. "Bob, I thought we had only four samples. When did we add a fifth bar?"

"I made one last night at home. We didn't have everything I needed downstairs in the test kitchen."

"That's hard to believe." Debbie rolled her eyes as she thought of the kitchen's vast array of ingredients. "But you're the expert, Bob. What's in the new bar?"

"Well, let's see how you like it first." He was like a kid bringing home a school project, eager for affirmation.

The team began passing around samples and taking notes. Burton leaned in to Paul and whispered in his ear, "Where's Gary? I expected him to be here."

Paul looked surprised. "He said he had a meeting off-site but that he'd be back. I guess I expected you to know."

Burton tried to be casual; he didn't want to alarm Paul. "I'm sure whatever he's doing is important to the project. Thanks," he said, thumping Paul once on his back. *This isn't OK. What's going on?*

Burton tried to clear his mind for the moment and focus on the samples. As hard as they had all worked, Burton found himself thinking that none of these new ideas really stood out. As they got to the last sample, Burton could see Bob's arms begin to wave ever so slightly and his grin grow wider. *This must be Bob's secret recipe*, he thought. Burton took a bite of the sample. It was, without a doubt, the most flavorful and interesting one of the bunch.

"Wow," said Burton. "You've been holding out on us, Bob. I really like this one." Burton saw Bob's arms begin a full swing. His napkin was sent flying off the table as he looked at Burton with a triumphant smile.

"That's the one I made last night. I *knew* you'd like it."

"I love it. OK," Burton called out, clapping his hands together twice, "let's take our top three choices and have the rest of the staff sample them. I think we all have a strong preference here, but let's get a little more feedback."

Bob's secret bar recipe became the clear favorite. The room was energized. Even Fred had ambled over to the sample table to participate. But Burton couldn't stop thinking about Gary.

On the way back to his office, Burton stopped at Gail's desk. "Would you send Gary in when he gets back? I need to talk to him as soon as possible."

Gail looked confused. "I don't think he was planning to be back for a few days."

"Back from where?" Burton asked, now feeling quite anxious.

"Burton, he's on his way to that meeting with Brigham Air." She sounded surprised that he didn't seem to know about it.

"What meeting with Brigham Air?"

"He's got a dinner scheduled with Susan Jenson, I believe."

"What? Dinner? You're kidding!" He felt a lump form in the back of his throat. *Something's up. Something's not right.*

"He set it up himself... I thought you knew. He said it was urgent."

"We're not ready to present to Brigham—at *all*. I'm not sure what he's doing meeting with them." Burton leaned heavily on her desk, considering what Gail had just told him.

"Since you named him project coordinator, I didn't think to run it by you."

"I understand, Gail. Of course. When did he leave?" He stood up straight and looked at the clock.

"About two hours ago. I'm sure he's in the air by now."

Burton felt his temple begin to throb as he went into his office. Contacting Mike, meeting with Brigham Air—Gary had apparently been a very busy man. *So, this was what he's been doing putting in all those extra hours.* Burton couldn't understand Gary's secrecy. *Why is he jumping the gun? We aren't ready to approach Brigham Air. What's he doing?*

"Hey Gary, this is Burton." He had reached Gary's voicemail. "I'd like you to contact me as soon as possible. I understand you have a meeting with Susan Jenson. I'm a little concerned and, frankly, quite confused. I think this meeting may be premature. Call and let me talk to you before you meet with Susan. Consider it urgent, please." Burton set the phone down softly as Gail walked in.

"Are you OK, Burton?"

"Did Gary say anything else before he left?"

"He asked for several copies of the latest presentation draft. He wanted them printed in full color and bound. That took a good chunk out of our printing budget, you know."

"Did he go through the travel desk to make the arrangements?"

"Actually, he didn't. He said it was so last minute that he'd make his own arrangements."

"Thanks, Gail." Burton watched Gail head back to her desk and tried to stay calm. He knew he wouldn't hear from Gary anytime soon. He yanked open his desk drawer where he kept all his notes on the airline project—his haphazard pile of "originals"—and his diary. They were *gone*. The reality and enormity of what Gary had done began to sink in. *That's it. It's all gone. You, my friend, have just been played. You gave it away, damn it. You gave it away.*

All he could think to do was escape—to get out of the office. He needed to think. *Just sell them bars, boy... We've got so much more to lose.* He could hear his father's voice and Julie's, taunting and indicting him, in turn. He snatched his briefcase and fled his office.

"Gail, tell the production team to guard the new sample recipes with their lives. And tell security not to let Gary Masters within an inch of the building." Mercifully, the elevator came quickly. *Escape.*

"Burton, are you alright?" Gail was up and in front of her desk.

"I'm out of here, Gail. Let everyone know I am out of the office today. I'll be back…but I don't know when."

The elevator doors shut between them, and he was gone.

Chapter 11

A Dream Destroyed

It is more tolerable to be refused than deceived.
—Publilius Syrus

THE RIDE DOWN THE ELEVATOR seemed interminable. Burton was sick to his stomach, light-headed. Sitting behind the wheel of his car, he wasn't sure where he wanted to go. *I can't believe this. Just when I feel like I'm seeing my vision finally taking shape, Gary pulls the rug out from under me. That bastard. I thought Fred was my problem, but Fred would never sell me out like this.*

I trusted him. How could I be so blind, so stupid? Where did I lose focus? Why is it that my ideas, my dreams, never quite come together? I'm so good at making things work for everyone else. He cringed as the full weight of what had been stolen began to settle in. It didn't matter if he still had a great bar recipe. Gary had the plan, Burton's *diary*, all their hard work, laid out in spreadsheets, charts, diagrams. Every i was dotted and every t crossed. It was all brilliant. Of course, Brigham Air would jump on it—and with multi-million-dollar airline horsepower, they would be miles ahead of anything Hall's could put together in the meantime.

Julie. Oh, Julie. He sat behind the wheel, his heart racing. He dialed his wife's cell number. She knew it was him. "Hey, honey. What's up?"

He hesitated. *Where do I even begin?* "Julie…it's gone."

"*What's* gone? What are you talking about Burton?" She was obviously concerned.

In fits and starts, Burton explained what had happened. "Burton!" Julie exclaimed. Then she was quiet. He knew she was probably surrounded by people. He heard her saying something to someone else, then footsteps, then quiet in the background. Finally, he heard her voice again. "What are you saying, Burton? Are you saying that the money we invested, from the Hall's account… Are you telling me that it's all down the drain?" There was another brief pause. "Burton you said you would be *careful.*" He could hear her begin to cry. "What do we…? Burton, why couldn't *you* just have bought yourself a Mustang of your own, or gone to Vegas, or gone skydiving, or…*something*?"

A midlife crisis. She thinks this was some midlife crisis. Coming from her, that was a kick in the stomach. He had wanted her support. He had wanted her to have faith in him. He had wanted her to be excited, even. *But she's right. I wanted more. It was wrong to want more. It was greedy, too risky.* He felt as though he'd failed—at the one thing he felt was really his. And he'd hurt Julie in the process. His father was right. *Just sell them bars, boy.* It was more than he could bear. "Julie, I won't be home for dinner tonight. I need to get away somewhere—to think things through."

She realized how upset he was, how her words must have stung. "Burton, please don't. I'm sorry, honey. It's just… Please just come home and let's talk about this together. It's going to be fine."

"Julie, I need some space right now. Don't worry about me. I'll be fine. I'll call you when I know what I'm doing."

"Burton, honey, I love you. So much. You know I do, right?"

"Yes, I do. I love you, too. I'll be OK. Please, just let me do this." Burton heard her sniffling a little, but she had stopped crying. She sounded OK. He was relieved.

"OK. Whatever you need. Whatever you need. Just please talk to me soon."

"I will." He hung up. As he pulled the car out of the parking lot, he saw the Miss Munchie logo, smiling and waving on the sign at the end of the lot: "Thanks for visiting Munchieville! Come back soon!" It mocked him. He turned toward the freeway.

He still felt sick to his stomach. He reviewed the last few months in his mind: the chance meeting with Susan, the excitement it stirred, the ideas that seemed to flow so easily, the connections that seemed to fit together so well. He thought of the great contact Mike Collier had been. He'd been solid, insightful, dependable—and the one who had suggested they sign a confidentiality agreement. *Life's little ironies*, Burton thought, comparing Mike's approach with Gary's. He'd have to let Mike know what had happened—soon. Gary had signed the company confidentiality agreement, but now that he had Burton's original notes, a breach would be hard to prove. He might argue that Burton had stolen *his* idea and back his claim using his dated e-files. Burton had always done his best thinking with low-tech paper and pen, and now he was paying for it.

Then he thought of Julie. He pictured her face that night they had talked in the kitchen. He remembered her alarm, her caution. He'd gotten her blessing and then let her down. And now what? He supposed he'd have to go back to pushing Miss Munchie bars, and pushing them *hard* to recoup monies that had gone into developing the airline idea. He winced. He'd been trying to escape it, but now he'd be knee-deep in Munchieville with little right to complain. *The staff. What will they think of all this? What will they do?* The team had invested so much time in this project. Would they lose respect for Burton or pin the blame squarely on Gary? What would this do to company morale?

Burton's thoughts were interrupted by the alarm sounding on his PDA, which lay on the passenger seat. *Damn. I thought I turned that off.* He picked it up and glanced at the screen long enough to see that Gary had sent him an e-mail. *This oughta be good.* He pulled over to the shoulder to read it. "Burton, I'm in Chicago. I'll be back on Thursday. We will have a lot to talk about. Gary." Burton stared at the message, sullen and angry. Even now, when he had clearly betrayed his boss, Gary was playing games—maybe still trying to cover all his bases. Burton decided to try to call him. The phone rang several times before Gary, in a hushed voice, answered. Burton was half surprised he picked up.

"Burton! Hey...let me call you back. I'm in the middle of a meeting."

"See, that is *exactly* why I'm calling. What are you doing out there...*buddy*?"

Gary whispered quietly. "Excuse me, I need to take this." Clearly, Gary now realized Burton was on to him. After a long pause, Gary sighed into the phone, "Burton, we really should meet to discuss this face to face when I get back on Thursday."

"I don't think you want your face anywhere near me, Gary." Burton's voice was icy.

"Alright, Burton." Gary drew in a long breath and let it out. "Look, Susan Jenson made me a very attractive offer, which I have accepted. I'm going to lead their catering and meal service development. They are going to develop a product in-house instead of looking for an outside supplier.

"In-house, huh? With *my* idea and strategy, with *my* inside employee. It's interesting that they call that *in-house*. Sounds a lot like bad business to me."

"Burton, you would have done the same thing if you were in my shoes," Gary said defensively.

"Not on your life, Gary. I don't run my company that way—I don't run my life that way. I mean, our wives are *friends*. Making a career move is one thing. Going behind my back and taking my idea with you is another stunt altogether."

"I'm sorry you feel this way."

"Feel? *Feel*? Well, I *feel* betrayed because I *was* betrayed. This isn't a difference of opinion, Gary. Hell, this is legally actionable. You stole my strategy—*my* idea."

"Burton, I can appreciate that you're upset, but don't forget all the work *I* did on this."

"Most of it behind my back. And don't forget whose payroll you were on, Gary!"

"This is business, Burton, not the school playground."

Burton couldn't believe what he was hearing. He didn't want to indulge Gary any further. "We'll pack your things and have them sent to your house. Your resignation is effective immediately." Burton hung up. Then he sent Gail an e-mail: "Notify personnel. Gary Masters is no longer with the company. I'm taking a couple days off. Hold the fort."

Burton thought back to the conversation he'd had with George at the Snack Expo. *This business is awash with Tater*

Tot terrorists waiting to steal from you and beat you to market, George had said, adamant that strategic ideas should be kept to oneself. Burton's heart sank at the realization that George's cynical perspective appeared to be right. He dialed Mike Collier and gave him the abridged version of the sordid tale.

"Burton, that's awful. I'm sorry. Will you sue?" Mike sounded genuinely concerned.

"Probably not, Mike. I don't know that there's much point. He walked away with my original notes, the whole game plan," Burton admitted somewhat sheepishly, "and we're not in a position to take on any legal bills right now. And that kind of press might hurt Miss Munchie's 'good girl' image." He laughed, despite his dark mood.

"Well, let me know if there's anything I can do. Chin up. You're one of the good guys out there. Things will work out for you, I'm sure."

"Like riding off into the sunset? Or 'happily ever after'?" Burton was sarcastic, but still trying to be upbeat.

"Giddyup, my friend," Mike replied gently.

The two men committed to stay in touch. Burton dialed one more number. Julie picked up right away.

"Where are you? Are you OK?"

"I'm headed to Ferguson's for a day or two. I'm hoping the fresh air, slower pace, and view will help me clear my head. I don't want you to worry."

"Are you sure you're OK?" Julie paused and then went on. "I'm sorry about all this. It's not your fault, you know. I know it's not your fault."

"Thanks. Yeah, I guess I know that, but so much was at stake in this for me. Sure I'm angry, but most of all I'm feeling lost right now." He tried to lighten the mood, mostly for her sake.

"I guess I'm going away to 'find myself'!" he laughed, trying to assure her that he was OK. She laughed too. He was relieved.

"You do what you need to do, then. But I'll be thinking of you. Please stay in touch."

"I will," he promised. "Love you."

After they hung up, Burton turned back onto the highway. He felt a little more relief with every mile he put between himself and the city. He arrived at his destination in the early evening. He hadn't eaten for several hours, but he wasn't hungry. He was happy just to be there, at this refuge that had become a second home. The cabins were lined up in cheery rows, standing at attention before the stunning view of the lake. Inside, their '50s-era tidiness harked back to a simpler time. There were nicer places to stay, but Ferguson's Motel and Diner had become a Hall family tradition. He and Julie had discovered the place on their honeymoon, when the nightly rate of $29.50 seemed like a luxurious splurge for a young couple with college loans. They'd tried other local places over the years, but they always came back to this little motel with its inviting rooms and amazing views.

When Mrs. Ferguson had learned that Julie was a fussy vegetarian and quite the chef, she invited Julie into her kitchen. She'd get the odd traveler looking for a satisfying meatless menu item, but she'd been raised to cook hearty meat and potatoes (or rice and pasta on occasion) in a dozen different ways. On a rainy afternoon in 1985, Julie's butternut squash soup was given a permanent spot on the diner menu—a beacon of health among the greasy-spoon fare. High-thread-count sheets and spa tubs could never compete with a bowl of soup on the porch near the pine tree that had grown from a seedling since the year Charlie was born.

Burton felt some of the day's tension ease as he sat on the porch, watching the sun slip into the horizon. The view pulled Burton's thoughts away from Gary's underhanded antics, but not for long. This would have been an amazing day. It should have been. The taste test and Bob's mystery recipe had been a great success. He would never have imagined that morning that a few short hours later he'd be sitting on this lonely porch wondering where to go from here.

Chapter 12

Hugo

> All men dream, but not equally. Those who
> dream by night in the dusty recesses of
> their minds, wake in the day to find that it was
> vanity: but the dreamers of the day are dangerous
> men, for they may act their dream with open eyes,
> to make them possible.
> —T. E. Lawrence

FIRST THING IN THE MORNING, Burton headed for the familiar little diner at the end of the row of quaint cottages. He was famished. Terry-Lee Ferguson, the unrelentingly chipper waitress and owner, greeted Burton as he walked in. She pulled a cup off the rack and poured him a coffee just as he sat down. She seemed ageless, but must have been running the place for at least 35 years. "Where's Julie and the kids?" she asked.

"I'm on my own this time—with Julie's blessing. Needed a getaway, someplace quiet where I could think—and just remember what it feels like to breathe again!" Burton stirred his coffee.

"In that case, you'll want the breakfast Julie won't let you order."

"You read my mind. Bacon and eggs and toast with butter. I want as much grease and salt as humanly possible. Hit me."

"You'll get heartburn. Remember last time you fell off the wagon?"

"A guy has to live dangerously once in a while," smiled Burton.

Terry-Lee nodded in agreement and called Burton's order into the kitchen: "Heart attack, over easy. Extra bacon."

Burton took a long draw of the fresh coffee. "Where's Pete? Fishing this morning?"

"He's got one of those man tests at the doctor's office. You'd think he was going to his death this morning. Constant complaining!"

Burton sputtered his coffee in surprise. "Well, how's that for too much information! Poor guy. Have you told all the customers about his 'man test'?"

"He didn't even know he had a prostrate gland before the doc told him," she laughed as she wiped the countertop. "I told him to just deal with it. Women have been doing exams we don't like for years. Still…" She looked at the gleaming countertop and then at Burton, her hands clutching the dish towel.

"Is everything OK?"

"We'll see. I think so. Those doctors know how to give people little scares, you know. I guess it serves to remind us what's important."

What's important? I need to be reminded. "I'm sure he'll be fine." Burton said gently.

"He'll have a pole in the water by noon, no doubt. Never misses a chance to fish this time of year."

Burton smiled as Terry-Lee swept through the diner to fill coffee cups and chat with customers. She slid his breakfast in front of him with the easy grace of a seasoned waitress. "Knock yourself out," she said. "I won't tell Julie. But don't make a habit of it. Julie thinks you're pretty darned important too. That's why she pesters you about what you eat."

"I know you're right. Wouldn't have it any other way." Burton picked up a piece of toast and savored the butter melting on the warm, crisp bread. Quietly skimming the newspaper, he tried to focus on the delicious flavors and the news of the day, hoping to distract himself from work and the anger that clung to him. The diner slowly emptied of customers, the breakfast rush over. Sounds of the kitchen and the tinny radio playing country music permeated the air.

His stomach full and spirits lifted, if only slightly, by the banter with Terry-Lee, Burton headed to the local General Store and Bait Shop to pick up some lake attire. His Miss Munchie ensemble didn't exactly help him blend into the surroundings. He took his purchases—cargo shorts, a Gone Fishin' T-shirt, and yellow flip-flops—back to his cabin to change. *I'm like a brand new man*, he thought. *Who are you kidding? You're stuck in the same old rut. Right back at square one.* Quickly growing restless, he decided to go for a walk along the lakeshore. Maybe the fresh air and exercise would help.

The flimsy flip-flops made him feel awkward, but he pressed on anyway, following the snaking shoreline. There were spots where the terrain was more broken, and he had to be careful navigating, but even that small challenge felt good. Apart from an occasional rustle in the brush and some birds chattering overhead, it was quiet. The lake was placid, serene. A few lonely fishermen in rowboats were on the lake, but everything was still. The slightest breeze wrinkled the surface of the water near the shore, but no ripples broke. Burton felt refreshed.

He'd been walking, or ambling, for about three-quarters of an hour when he came to an old pier jutting out into the lake. It clearly wasn't used for watercraft anymore. The wood was weathered and broken in several places, and what had been a path from the pier up the gently rising embankment was now mostly overgrown. At the end of the pier, about 50 feet offshore, sat a lone figure in a deckchair. He was wearing a green golf shirt, khaki shorts, and open sandals. Beside him sat a well-worn wicker tackle basket, and his head was covered by a paint-splattered hat. Burton was close enough to see that the hat was decked not with lures or flies, but with tourist pins—and the man wasn't fishing. He was leaning forward, and then sitting back, in a slow, steady rocking motion, moving from his chair back to the canvas on the easel in front of him. Curious and feeling like he wanted some company, Burton started onto the pier.

The artist felt the rise and fall of the pier with Burton's footsteps and turned to see who his visitor was. He called out, "Hello," smiling and shielding his eyes with his free hand. When Burton reached him, the man didn't wait for introductions. "You plan on fishing today?" he asked, though Burton was clearly empty-handed.

"Uh, no sir."

"There's more than fish to catch around here, you know. Me, I'm trying to catch a vision of this place, one moment captured on canvas. Or, I guess," he mused to himself, "I'm letting it catch me." He chuckled and reached for a thermos by his side. "Care for some lemonade? I always bring an extra cup—just in case."

"Sure," Burton heard himself answer. This man seemed odd, but he was somehow captivating. He took the lemonade gratefully and poured half the glass down the back of his throat. It was cool, not too sweet—just what he needed.

"Unfortunately, I can't manage the extra chair..."

"The pier's fine." Burton sat down and folded his legs under himself as best he could. *I've got to get more exercise. I'm not as limber as I used to be.* The man reached into his tackle box for some more paint. "First time up here?" Burton asked.

"No sir," the artist replied. "Nope. I'm just here living the dream, so to speak." He looked amused with himself.

"Oh, you've retired up here, then?" Burton asked.

"Retired, but not here. I move around a lot. My dream's bigger than just retirement, my friend." He smiled knowingly. Burton wondered if this guy was all there. He seemed harmless enough.

"Oh, and what dream is that?" He couldn't hide his cynicism.

"*Mine*," the artist replied, like a small child grabbing back a stolen ball.

Burton ventured cautiously. "Dreams are a tricky business," he sighed. "They don't always go according to plan."

"That's true. It's easy to get off track. But when it's right..." His voice trailed, and his heavily lined face looked peaceful and happy.

"So, what is it you're dreaming up, if I may ask?" Burton shifted, pulling his knees up to his chest. He felt like a small boy sitting at his father's side.

"Oh, it's a long story."

"I have time if you do," Burton said. "That is, if you don't mind telling it."

"Well, don't say I didn't warn you," he grinned. "Us old farts can get a little long-winded, you know. I'm Hugo, by the way." He extended his hand.

"Burton. Nice to meet you."

Hugo seemed to study Burton's face for a moment, collecting his thoughts while he considered the man sitting next to him.

"I'm a portrait painter. Been doing it for over 35 years. My brother and I went into business together. He did all the sales and marketing. I just painted. We were a very successful team."

"That must be interesting work," Burton interjected.

"It is. I was lucky to be doing something I enjoyed, and I got to meet some fascinating people. But 35 years of just portraits is a long time. When I was young, I never imagined I'd make my living this way. Eventually, I started going back to those old dreams I'd had. They were always in my mind. It was strange, dreaming about painting landscapes while painting portraits of rich people."

"Strange? In what way?" Burton leaned in. Hugo's face was rapt with quiet happiness, remembering something wonderful. "It's a long story…" His voice trailed off again, almost dreamily. He sat quietly for a moment before turning to Burton. "I had this old canvas in my studio for over 20 years. I'd saved it for that first landscape I always hoped I'd get to paint one day. Commission after commission came in for portraits, and I just never had time—you know how it is."

"I do," said Burton. "It's amazing how easy it is to get wrapped up in one thing, doing the same thing over and over again. So did you get a chance to paint your landscape?"

"I did. I'd had a terrible year. My brother had a heart attack, and I lost my wife to cancer. She was my sweetheart—best thing that ever happened to me." He looked down at the wooden slats beneath his feet. "You might imagine how a thing like that could give a man perspective."

"I'm sure it would."

"I had a stack of jobs I didn't want to do, and finally I'd had enough. I looked at that old canvas stuck in the corner, gathering dust, and I just said, 'The hell with it, I'm going to do it.' I was in Tuscany 20 hours later. Best damn thing I ever did. I haven't painted a portrait since."

"What was so special about Tuscany?" Burton inquired.

"My mother was born there, and she used to tell us kids stories of how she grew up. It sounded like a magical place, and her stories were so bright and full of life, fun, and family. Growing up in upstate New York wasn't like that. My life as a kid was hard. Sometimes I'd take off, find a hill to sit on, and dream of what it would have been like to have been a boy growing up in Tuscany, the way my mother described it, to be able to play hide and seek in a vineyard. I didn't like my landscape, I suppose." He laughed a little and offered Burton some more lemonade, which he took happily.

"You get to Tuscany back then?" Burton asked.

"No. A car crash took my mother when I was very young. Life got harder. Imagining where she grew up, in that warm Tuscan landscape—that became my way of connecting with her. And disconnecting with the real world some too. I decided never to go because I didn't want to take the chance that what I was imagining, that landscape I had in my mind, wasn't real after all. I needed to cling to that image, no matter what."

Hugo sighed. He went on, "When my wife died, well, it was losing the only woman I'd ever loved—after my mother, that is. That vision of Tuscany was more than just a dream; it was a landscape that my mother and I had created together. A few days later, I was sitting in my and my brother's studio painting yet another portrait. I kept looking at that old canvas in the corner, staring at that blank canvas. Blue skies and sunny villas flashed on that canvas like a Tuscan slideshow. I was grounded to the present, painting portrait after portrait. I was living out my brother's dream and not my own—it was as false as that image of Tuscany I had conjured in my mind. That canvas leaning against the wall and the dream attached to it were the only things in that moment that were real, that were truly mine. So I decided to go to Tuscany to find a landscape of my own, and I was going to capture it on canvas and make it real…and make it really mine. I was going to make it—along with my memory of my mother and my wife—something I could hold on to."

Burton and Hugo sat quietly, both surprised at how honest and candid the conversation had turned. Hugo's smile told Burton that he enjoyed telling this story; he had a perceptible, gentle pride as he spoke, the pride of experience and endurance. Burton was glad to think about someone else's life for a change. "Did you find that Tuscan landscape?"

"Yep. Almost immediately. I found an old bridge over a winding brook, nestled in an old vineyard. It was perfect. It captivated me. And it reminded me of the stories my mother would tell of when she was young and free. Every day for six weeks I painted that bridge on that old canvas. I've never felt so alive. I know it may sound strange, but I had tears in my eyes much of the time. I expected to enjoy the work, and I knew it was a special project. I guess I never expected to feel so renewed. I was painting with my heart—not for a paycheck. That's when I became a *real* artist, I think."

"So no more portraits?"

"Not a one. That one landscape turned into something much bigger. The dream's gone global, I guess you could say," he laughed.

"What do you mean?"

"I went back home and kept visiting the friends Marg made in the cancer ward. Some people think that's depressing, but not me. There are some well-lived lives in that place and lots of great stories. I kept hearing story after story from the patients there: stories about childhood antics, school accomplishments, wedding days, special family memories of both joy and loss. They'd talk about people and places, and I'm not sure how it happened, exactly, but I kept imagining the landscapes they were talking about. So to make a long story short, what I do now is take those people's stories, and I put them on canvas—create a memory. I get a description from a patient of a memory of a special place, sometimes an old photo to help, and I go find that spot. Then, I paint it. After, I come back with the painting to give to that person. They can hang that memory on the wall, stare at it, live in it. It's a conversation starter for sure.

"The hospital's developed a program called 'Magic Memories.' The families of my 'clients' donate my work back to the hospital. Then the paintings get auctioned once a year at a special charity event to raise money for cancer research. It's changing lives, I know." He gestured to the painting in front of him and pulled out a photo of a young man who'd lost most of his hair. Burton guessed he was about 30. "This is Adam. He wanted me to come here and paint this spot. He told me how he and his dad used to come here on special fishing trips when he was a teenager. He told me how they used to see who could throw stones or spit the farthest. Nice kid." He nestled the photo carefully back into his tackle box. "Money goes to cancer research, I get to do one of my favorite things—travel—and those people who pass away after their illness live on in someone's living room or bedroom, bringing inspiration. Right now, there are little pieces of those folks' dreams, alive and well, on walls all over the Northwest! And I can't think of a better way to honor the memory of my wife and mother."

"Wow. That's amazing. Your story makes me wish I could paint." Burton laughed. "I'd be on the next plane to Tuscany!"

"My wife used to say that everybody can paint a landscape. It's just painters who are limited by brushes and oils. We all make pictures in our own way. We create our own special landscapes. She was right, I think."

"I'm still trying to figure out what my landscape is," said Burton, "or if it's even worth painting."

"Don't give up. The whole damn world is out of practice, if you ask me. I know I was. It took me near a lifetime to figure it out. I wonder how many landscapes are out there that never get painted," Hugo said wistfully. "How many ideas go untested? How many dreams just lie dormant? Keep dreaming, son," he said, turning to face Burton. "But remember..." Hugo paused, as though he were about to give Burton a precious coin. "The best dreams are the ones that inspire others to dream right along with you. Dreams should add something to the world, not take anything away from it. They have to be about more than our own little existence, or they're not really dreams at all—they're just goals. And yes, there is a difference. Sometimes they start in the same place, though."

"You seem to be following your own advice," said Burton.

"I try to. Once you start, it gets easier."

Burton stood and stretched. As much as he had escaped the office, he felt compelled to go back to his cabin to check his PDA. He also wanted some time to chew on what Hugo had told him. Hugo reached into his tackle box, pulled out his business card, and handed it to Burton. The title under his name was "Memory Painter." Burton, obviously unprepared to be doing business lakeside, didn't have a card to offer in return.

Hugo looked Burton straight in the eye, his gaze piercing, yet warm, under his bushy gray eyebrows. "You go dream that dream and then make it come true. Then I want you to call me and tell me all about it. You understand now?"

Burton just nodded and smiled silently, extending his hand. Hugo bypassed Burton's hand and gave him a slap on the back that nearly knocked him off his feet. Offering thanks for the refreshment—both the lemonade and conversation—Burton said goodbye and made his way back along the pier to the shore. With his hands in his pockets, he trudged back the way he came and turned Hugo's tale over in his mind. He could relate to the old man's sense of being stuck in his brother's studio, painting one portrait after another, while feeling restless for something else. "Everybody paints," Hugo had said.

What am I painting? Paint-by-numbers, he thought, laughing to himself. *Every color and line is laid out for me. I just fill things in to complete the picture. Someone else's picture. Do I have my own landscape? Do I even have a dream?* He was struck by the contrast between Gary and Hugo. Gary's patronizing "This is business, Burton," and Hugo's "Dreams should add something to the world, not take anything away from it." *What about me? Am I doing "business as usual," or am I adding something to the world?* He went over his airline idea. It met a need, for sure. Everyone he knew complained of airline food service, but was he thinking big enough? *If the sky is the limit, is 30,000 feet reaching high enough?* He wasn't sure what to make of it all.

He suddenly felt overwhelmed—and hungry. He made his way back to Ferguson's Diner.

Chapter 13

Same Dream, New Landscape

> Knowing trees, I understand
> the meaning of patience.
> Knowing grass, I can appreciate persistence.
> —Author unknown

AFTER TWO NIGHTS at the cabin, Burton was ready to head home. He didn't know how much more alone time he could take. He missed Julie and the kids, and he'd gone round and round in his mind, over and over everything that had happened at work during the past several months, Gary's betrayal, and Hugo's captivating story. Burton couldn't let go of the sense that their meeting hadn't been accidental. But what was he to make of it? *Maybe I should just be grateful for the peek into the life of someone who's living his dream. It is possible after all. Maybe it's worth hoping that I can have that sense of fulfillment and purpose some day.*

He'd gone through the options of where he could go from here. He kept coming back to Munchieville with discouragement and some resignation, but, he had to admit, there was a little bit of hope there too. Maybe Maximum Bob's stroke of genius in the kitchen could become a new hit in the Miss Munchie lineup. Maybe that would be enough of a change of pace—having something new to create and market. *Maybe...maybe not.*

It didn't take long before Burton had loaded his things into the car and was on his way down the highway. When he'd called Julie to tell her he'd be home the next day, she sounded relieved. He was eager to see her. More than anything, he just wanted to enjoy some time with her, talking about anything but business. The idea of adding a new bar to the Miss Munchie line was still one he wanted to bring up with her, but he was more than happy to let it sit for at least a day.

He was on his way home, back to his family, but also back to Munchieville and the same predictable routine. He knew he'd have to explain to the rest of the staff what had happened with Gary. They'd probably feel let down. He was embarrassed. How would he account for being so easily fooled? Fred would be relentless, shaking his head and offering at least one glibly self-assured "I told you so." Maybe the idea of a new bar could sustain some of the momentum in the staff, at least until he could figure out what it was he really wanted, a dream that really mattered. *What am I painting? It's definitely abstract art at this point.*

The gas gauge needle was nearly on empty, so Burton began looking for a place to refuel. He pulled off into the town of Cloverdale, with its six-block main street. Some of the storefronts were generations old; others were newer. He pulled into a service station with a small convenience store. After filling the tank with gas, Burton went inside to pay and to grab something to drink and snack on. He made his way over to the refrigerators at the back of the store to see what would catch his eye. He soon noticed a thin, tired-looking woman, perhaps in her late 30s, placing some prepackaged submarine sandwiches into a small duffel bag. She looked at Burton and noticed that he was obviously wondering what she was up to. "I work here," she said, smiling and pointing to her name tag. It read "Molly." "I know this doesn't look good!"

Burton counted three sandwiches going into the tattered blue bag. "You must be hungry," he said, making conversation.

"Oh, they're not for me," she replied, taking Burton's good-natured joke literally. "They're past the 'best-before date' and the boss...well..." She paused a moment, studying Burton's face. He felt like she was sizing him up. "He lets me take them home if no one's bought them by then. He knows I'm on my own and this is the only job I have, so..." Her gaze fell to the bag and then away from Burton. He could see she was embarrassed.

"Here, let me help you, Molly. I'm Burton, by the way," he said quietly to reassure her. He helped her find and place the remaining dated sandwiches in her bag—six altogether. She thanked him.

"Now what?" Burton asked innocently.

Molly looked down at the bag and then into Burton's face, again searching it carefully. "Well," she said, "I'll go throw these in the cooler at the back and then take them home when my shift's over." She saw Burton's brow furrow. Brightly, she continued, "This is enough for the kids' school lunches for the week—or more." She saw the obvious look of dismay on Burton's face. "The sandwiches are fine, really. Maybe not the best, but..." she hesitated, "they're fine. The egg salad gets tossed, but the rest are just fine." She swung the bag over her shoulder and started toward the door to the back of the shop. "Thanks for your help," she said. "I'll be back in a jiff to give you a hand." She disappeared from sight for a few minutes.

Expired sandwiches? Burton could hardly believe it. He supposed they'd still be alright after a day or two, but to eat them over a week or more? He knew they were chock full of preservatives and fat—a lot of empty calories. Shuddering, he imagined the wilted lettuce and chemically whitened bread made soggy by mayonnaise. Julie would be horrified.

Molly came out from the back of the store. Burton took his bottle of juice and a bag of peanuts to the counter and waited for her to come around to the till. "I hope you don't mind my asking, but how many kids do you have, Molly?"

She smiled as if eager to talk about her children. "There's Bobby, who's 11, Rachel, who's just turned 9, and Ollie, who'll be 7 in the fall."

"They go to school here in Cloverdale?"

"No. But they all go to the same school, lucky for me—in Lost Hills. They get bussed in and out. They're great kids." She couldn't hide her pride. She rang up his purchase.

Burton thanked her. He hesitated for a moment and then reached into his wallet to pull out a well-worn $100 bill. "You know, I've had this kicking around for a while. For about a year I've wanted to find a good way to dispose of it—maybe hand it off to someone who'd make good use of it. I don't need it, and it sounds like you've got your hands full. Maybe little Ollie could use a new toy?"

Molly blushed and looked down. She shook her head. "No... no, I couldn't. There's folks who need it more than I do. Thanks all the same though. You're very kind, but I couldn't." She smiled shyly.

"You're sure?" Burton pressed. The phone started to ring.

She slid over to where it was, looking torn, as though she didn't want to be rude to Burton.

"You go ahead. I'll be on my way."

"You have a safe trip home or to wherever you're headed. And thanks again for your kindness." She gave Burton a big smile and then reached for the phone. She answered it cheerily.

While she was distracted, Burton folded the $100 bill and tucked it carefully under the edge of the till and toward Molly, where she'd be sure to see it after she'd finished with her call. Burton took his purchases and slipped out of the store.

Walking back to his car, he felt he needed to do something more for this woman. He jotted down the address of the gas station and determined to send her some boxes of Miss Munchie bars. They weren't a meal, but at least they were a good healthy snack, and her kids would probably like them, maybe even the boys. Burton turned the key in the ignition and then froze as he was struck by a thought. *Wait a minute. What if...?* He heard Hugo's words: *Dreams should add something to the world... What if I could do better than an airline meal replacement? What if I could invest in something bigger, something more important?* His mind was racing—much like it had started racing after his conversation with Susan at the Snack Expo, only this time it was better. *What if Maximum Bob's wonder bar could become a healthy, delicious meal for kids in schools? Julie. I have to call Julie.* He dialed her quickly and told her what he was thinking. It was good to hear her voice. She was glad to hear his too. As he talked, she heard the spark again. More than that, she heard hope. Burton couldn't wait to get home. He pulled out onto the highway. It took every ounce of fortitude not to put the accelerator to the floor. He couldn't wait to get home and to his team at the office.

✧ ✧ ✧

Maximum Bob and his development team entered the conference room the next morning to find Burton already there, well into his second cup of coffee. "Here are the cookie monsters!" he exclaimed. The group sat down and looked at Burton expectantly. Bob, looking more disheveled than usual, stammered awkwardly, "Mr. Hall, we understand there is a problem regarding the airline project." Gail had kindly brought the team up to speed in Burton's absence. She'd known how hard it would be for him to face them alone. They'd been gracious, even Fred. They seemed to be rallying together against the injustice.

"Yes, there is a problem, and it's a big one. A disaster." He was grinning from ear to ear, delighted. The rest of the room was confused and a little alarmed. "But you aren't here to talk about that. I've got some new ideas, you see. Let's talk about cookies."

"Cookies, sir?" Even Maximum Bob thought Burton might have a screw loose.

"What if," Burton paced around the room, "we shift our focus to schools? They may be the perfect match for Bob's recipe anyway. School programs need something nutritious and easy to store and sell. We have a lot of research to do, but I'd like to investigate this angle and use the bar recipe to make a kid-friendly meal cookie."

"A meal cookie?" Debbie asked.

"It has to meet high nutritional standards, of course. But," he looked around at his small team with a grin, "that's what we're good at. I want it to be fun and really appeal to children. It has to taste great with one of those little cartons of milk."

"Sounds like a Doughgod," said Bob.

"A Doughgod? What on earth is a Doughgod, Bob?" asked Debbie.

"My grandfather used to make 'em. He's the man who taught me how to bake, you know." Bob's voice filled the small room. "Just about anything he baked was a Doughgod. He had Christmas and Easter Doughgods. We had a Doughgod for Halloween. I used to sort M&Ms for the eyes and mouths."

"I have absolutely no idea what you're talking about, Bob. But make some up—and more of your bars, too. Just alter them to look like cookies. I have a list here of approved ingredients for the national school lunch program. We have to limit ourselves to the list. You think you can make a Doughgod or two with this?" He handed Bob a sheet of paper.

Bob surveyed the list, stroking his chin. "It's not ideal, but it can be done. I'm not going to use half the crap they have on the list. It's a bunch of FDA-approved chemicals and junk, if you ask me."

"I *am* asking, Bob. I want it to be healthy. Instead of giving kids junk and pumping it full of preservatives while we're at it, I want to set a new standard."

"Well, I'll whip up a few *healthy* Doughgods, and we'll see what you think." Maximum Bob stood at attention as though he was taking orders.

"Our audience is kids, so keep it fun. By the way, I'd prefer to keep this idea quiet right now. We'll get a little further along before we announce it to everyone."

"We don't want another Gary on our hands," nodded Debbie. "What a slime ball."

"He gets wind of this, he'll be on the phone with the Girl Scouts plotting before the end of business hours," added Will Walker, production supervisor.

"I just want to handle this project differently," said Burton. "Besides, no one even knows what a Doughgod is. We're *all* working in the dark at this point."

"Just you wait," said Bob, his voice booming.

"It'll be top secret, Mr. Hall. 'Project Doughgod,' whatever that is." Debbie gave Burton an encouraging smile. "I really like the idea of doing something for the schools."

"Yep," nodded Bob, emphatically. "I'm excited by this. It feels right. My grandfather would be proud to know his Doughgod recipes would help kids. I love the idea."

"Me too," Burton said. "Feels like we're right back on track. No, it feels like we're finally on the *right* track."

Chapter 14

The Special Kneads Team

> Discovery consists of seeing
> what everybody has seen
> and thinking what nobody has thought.
> —Albert Szent Gyorgyi

WILL HAD ALWAYS HATED the pink and orange world of Munchieville. As the seasoned production supervisor, he performed his job with unrelenting focus and precision. Not a day went by, however, when he didn't think about how much the production line looked like Candyland. With a name like Will Walker, it hadn't taken long for the employees to dub him "Willy Wonka of Munchieville." As he worked on Burton's new project with Bob and Debbie, he worried that these "meal cookies" would mean he would once again be building his resume on products using cute colors and twirling fairies.

Will couldn't be less concerned with all the fuss and bustle in the test kitchen—he would take whatever they came up with and produce it to perfection. He'd wrap it neatly, package it for delivery, and ship it on time. He had worked with Fred for many years, and the two grumpy old men knew how to get a job done. He'd seen many Miss Munchie bars in his day and never expected Hall's to launch anything new. Creating something different was going to be a challenge—and a welcome one. Even if, he thought ruefully, it still came in a silly wrapper.

Will joined the rest of the newly formed Special Kneads team for an early morning meeting in the test kitchen. They had been working under the radar for days, still cautious after Gary's defection to Brigham Air. The team all wore white smocks and caps. Will knew a "Willy Walker in the Cookie Factory" joke was close at hand. Bob, in a smock, his black glasses, and red tennis shoes, smiled at Will as he walked in. "Hey Willy! You look like a grumpy old Oompa Loompa man!"

"Let's not go there, Bob." Will winced at Bob's booming voice so early in the morning. "I don't expect to see you on the cover of *Gentleman's Quarterly* anytime soon."

Burton watched his motley team begin their usual good-natured bickering. The group had been working closely all week, and an easy banter had developed between them. Burton had been delighted when Debbie tried to explain to Bob what an "inside voice" was. Bob seemed enormously pleased to see the team. Burton steeled himself for an enthusiastic response, silently praying that Debbie's lesson on vocal control had managed to sink in.

"Hey there, Mr. Hall," Bob boomed. "I have a batch just out of the oven. Let me get you a fresh one. Wait till you try these! I've gotten the recipe just right now."

Bob pulled a tray of large cookies out of the warming oven. "Ladies and gentlemen," he said with a flourish, "I give you the Doughgod. We have cinnamon spice, oatmeal trail mix, and chocolate brownie for you to sample today."

Burton looked at the moist, chocolate cookie. "That looks too good to be healthy, Bob."

"You know, Mrs. Hall actually helped me with that one. She added pumpkin and a little plum to replace the sugar. It turned out great and is real healthy."

"Julie was here?" Burton asked, surprised.

"She was here all day yesterday, when you were out doing taste tests at the golf course," quipped Bob. "She helped me get a few issues worked out, like protein and fiber content. She loves these things. She was excited to help, and she even thought of ways to add vegetables like carrots, zucchini, and"—he gulped—"broccoli without anyone even being able to taste 'em."

"Wow. I always knew Julie was something else, but that's amazing!" He was touched by her having been there, offering her insight and help with *his* idea. It meant a lot to him. "Well, let's eat!" Burton and the team began to try Bob's samples. Burton was amazed at how good each flavor was. Bob's Doughgods were moist and soft, loaded with fruit—and hidden vegetables. "Wow." Burton wiped a crumb off his lip. "These are really good."

"We've been working all week," said Bob. "We had to create a texture that would withstand the packaging process and a flavor sweet enough to appeal to kids, while using natural alternatives to refined sugar. Sure, this is batch one-hundred-and-something, but we finally got it right."

"This is more than 'right.' These are fantastic, Bob. Doughgods, huh?" Burton said, examining the cookie in his hand. "Well, I'm a believer."

"We got the moisture content just right," added Will. "They have been consistent, batch after batch, which is essential. We don't want these damn lumps to get hard or fall apart."

"Every ingredient is from the approved list. We have some other flavors we're still working up," Debbie said, with her mouth half full. She broke off another piece of the brownie cookie and popped it into her mouth. "There are so many allergies out there. We need a gluten-free option."

"How about a vegan cookie, too?" Will added. "My daughter and her friends all claim to be vegan these days. Whatever that means."

"V-gods. Grandpa is starting to roll over in his grave right now," lamented Bob, "but I guess we need a lot of variety. We're already looking into rice flours and soy products; the basic dough can be altered in a thousand ways. I started using those wheat flakes that Fred was griping and moaning about. Ever since he began working inventory, he's been after me to move that stuff out. It was a happy accident. I wouldn't have tried it, except that I wanted Fred off my back."

"Well, Fred is pretty fussy about the storeroom, I agree," Will smiled slowly at Bob, "but you have to admit it was a mess in there. Somebody has to be the bad guy."

"Well," said Bob, "for once I was glad Fred was his usual miserable self. Wheat flakes really made the difference."

"I think we have the basic concept here," said Burton. "You've all done amazing work. I'm really impressed." Burton's team beamed. Compliments rang out freely as the group drank coffee for a few minutes while nibbling at the remaining samples. The test kitchen smelled wonderful and inviting. Burton couldn't wait to share the samples with Julie and the kids.

He thought about Molly and the old sandwiches that found their way into her kids' lunchboxes. He loved knowing that he had a warm, filling, and healthy alternative, one that filled the kitchen with the aroma of wholesome but also delicious food.

This wasn't a cold, plastic-coated sandwich. This wasn't slick, greasy fast food. This was the difference between simply filling a child's stomach and really nourishing that child. Burton couldn't wait to send to Molly what was Hall's latest product, but what had turned into so much more. *The Doughgods must be smiling,* thought Burton.

"Let's find a school to adopt. We need to start a meal cookie giveaway. I want to see how these go over with the fussiest test market—kids."

"We need some packaging," said Will. "We haven't worked anything up yet."

"We need a name and logo, too," added Debbie. "No offense, Bob, but Doughgod may not be a name we want to use commercially."

"It's about kids," Burton interjected. "We should let kids help us with that part." He rubbed his chin thoughtfully and then slapped the table. "I have an idea! I'm going to get my daughter, Samantha, and maybe a few of her friends to work on the label and logo. I think a few 10-year-old girls have more insight on the young market than some crotchety old marketing bozo."

Two weeks later, Burton and Maximum Bob pulled into the parking lot of a nearby elementary school. It was no small task getting all the necessary paperwork and permission slips in order. School districts had a heavy set of rules and restrictions, especially for food. The district office moved slowly and cautiously, if at all. Burton realized that this was not a "business" in any sense of the word.

Gail had managed to navigate through most of the district hurdles, and a taste test had been scheduled for just after recess.

"This is gonna be so cool," Bob said as he unloaded the boxes from the car. "The Doughgods will be a hit."

"Bob, we can't call them Doughgods, remember?" said Burton.

"Yeah, yeah. Meal cookies. *Bor-ing.*"

"You can't have all the good ideas," Burton ribbed. "Did you bring the feedback forms?"

"Don't worry. I doubt we'll need 'em, but I got 'em."

"We're here for input, Bob. We need to run this professionally. This isn't the Great Cookie Giveaway."

"These things rock. Not much more to say."

Burton had to laugh at his optimistic head baker. He was obviously thrilled to share his recipe, and his enthusiasm was infectious. "I like your confidence, Bob. Let's go hand out some Doughgods! I mean meal cookies."

After getting visitors' passes, they made their way to the cafeteria. "Watch out, Mr. Hall," Bob said in his best indoor voice. "Every school has a lunch lady who's mean and crazy."

"Honestly, Bob." Burton rolled his eyes. "You really are a case, you know."

"Gentlemen!" A shrill voice rang out down the hallway. "Gentlemen! Passes, please! I need your passes, gentlemen!"

"Told you." Bob said, smirking. "Someone should tell her about her inside voice."

Burton handed over his hall pass for inspection. "My paperwork is in order, ma'am," he smiled. "We're headed to the cafeteria."

"We'll just see about that." The woman snatched the pass from Burton's hand and looked him up and down. "You are to report to the cafeteria. Let's move along."

"Uh...yeah. Let's move along, Bob." Burton suddenly felt

eight years old again. He and Bob walked into the cafeteria and began to set up the cookies and evaluation forms on the long tables. An older woman in a black hairnet supervised them with an eagle-eyed suspicion that prompted them to hurry. "I see what you mean, Bob," Burton whispered. "That lunch lady scares the hell out of me."

"*Shhhh*," Bob admonished. "I don't want to get in trouble."

"Right, let's go." They worked quickly.

"I wish we could watch the kids as they try the cookies."

"Me too," said Burton, "but the district wanted to supervise this themselves. Maybe we can observe the next round at another school."

An older man in a dark blue suit waltzed into the cafeteria just as Burton and Bob were set to leave. He paced up and down along the tables, eyeing the cookies, his hands clasped behind his back as he hummed softly. "Are these for the staff?" he asked hopefully.

"They're for the kids, actually," said Burton. "They'll be trying them this afternoon and then completing a survey. We're developing a new product for the school lunch program."

"Indeed. Indeed," the teacher said. "Looks good...looks good..." He ambled out the doorway and down the hall, continuing to hum and murmur to himself.

That afternoon, Burton and Hall's Special Kneads team placed a call in to the school, hoping to get a sense of how the cookies had gone over with the kids. Bob, Will, and Debbie sat around Burton's desk, eagerly waiting to see how the little Doughgods had fared in their first test. After a few minutes on hold, the principal, Jane McFee, greeted the team with a rather weary hello. "Mr. Hall," she sighed, "the students really had fun taking part in your taste test."

"Wonderful," said Burton. "I know we'll be picking up the surveys tomorrow, but we were wondering if you had an overall impression of how the test went. Did the students seem to enjoy the cookies?"

"Absolutely. The kids really seemed to like them. We were disappointed to run out of samples so soon."

"Run out?" Bob said, incredulous. "You had enough cookies for every student on campus and then some. There were over 500 cookies!"

"We had enough for the third- and fourth-graders, but only half of the fifth-grade class got to try them." She paused and added, irritated, "It certainly wasn't your fault, but we nearly had a riot on our hands when we ran out. It's wasn't pretty, let me tell you."

"I don't understand. What happened?" asked Burton. "Where did 200 cookies disappear to?"

"The black hole known as the teachers' lounge. Apparently, Mr. McDaniel helped himself after you left. There were empty trays and wrappers all over the place. The teachers plowed through a good number of cookies before recess was even over. I also discovered a few dozen stashed next to the coffee pot. I'm not surprised—you know how teachers are. The good news is, they really liked them too."

"I guess! Geez!" Bob rolled his eyes.

"You're welcome to come back and run the test with the fifth- and sixth-graders. The kids responded really well, and sales of milk were way up, so the cafeteria is happy. We'd love to see the meal cookies again. I promise to keep Mr. McDaniel under lock and key."

"Looks like we'd better bake extra for the staff this next time," said Burton.

"And the staff's children...and the secretary...parents...the custodian," said the principal. "I think your notion of extra and their notion of extra are two different things."

After the call ended, the team looked expectantly at Burton. "Well," he said, "despite the glitches today, it looks like the response was terrific. Good job, everyone."

"Look at it this way," laughed Debbie. "If they're worth stealing, they're worth eating, and it sure sounds like those teachers stole plenty of 'em."

Bob's arms had been swinging slightly, signaling incoming enthusiasm. Debbie and Will had unconsciously moved their chairs slightly away from the wild baker. "Told you, Mr. Hall!" Bob said, abandoning his inside voice. "Doughgods rule!"

Chapter 15

And the Survey Said...

> It's never just a game when you're winning.
> —George Carlin

A FEW DAYS LATER, Burton was back at the elementary school to collect the surveys. As he walked down the hallway to the principal's office, he noticed that the walls were plastered with student artwork, all depicting Hall's meal cookies.

"Where did all the artwork come from?" Burton asked as he walked into the office and shook Jane's outstretched hand.

"Well, the students and teachers wanted to say thank you. Everyone had a good time as a taste tester."

"That's fantastic. I did notice there was one drawing with Mr. McDaniel in jail."

"The kids learned about our cookie thief. They've been teasing him all week. If you look closely, you'll see he's in leg irons." She handed Burton a neat stack of evaluation forms. "I hope you don't mind, but the math teacher wanted the kids to tabulate the results. It created a nice real-world math lesson."

"Are you kidding? That's great!" Burton exclaimed. "So how'd we do?"

"Looks like you guys got 93 out of 100. Not bad at all." Jane handed Burton a neatly handwritten tally sheet. "That's an A."

"Wow." Burton had hoped for results in the 70s or low 80s. Feedback like this was far better than he'd expected. "The kids really liked them, then."

"So did the teachers, don't forget," Jane said. "And I should tell you, on many days, we have kids who are hungry again before recess. But not after they had your cookies. The cookies are surprisingly hearty."

"I'm glad to hear it went so well." Burton scanned the hallways again. "I'd like to take some of the artwork back, if I could. We've had an idea to use children's artwork for the label."

"The kids would love that! Be my guest," she said.

Burton walked back to the car, his arms full of evaluation forms and artwork. Carefully, he loaded the papers into the trunk and headed back to the plant. His daughter and her friends had been drawing all week. He knew children's artwork could be a big part of the product's success. Perhaps different packaging for each grade level would work. And maybe they could have a little contest each year, with the winner's artwork being used on the packaging for a year. He wanted to brainstorm and let more ideas come forward. He phoned home, and Sam answered. "Hall residence," she said.

"Hey there, sweetie. Nice job answering the phone. Very businesslike."

"Daddy! I just got home from school. Charlie picked me up."

"Did you have a good day?"

"I got an A on my spelling test. Well, an A–…or maybe it was actually a B+. *Really* close to an A!"

"That *is* pretty close," Burton agreed. Accuracy had never been his daughter's strong suit, but she could sure draw. "I need your help with something, Sam."

"Are we cleaning the garage again? I hate that, Dad."

"That may be next week. Listen, I know you and your friends have been working on artwork for me. I'd like to get all of your drawings together, maybe even do some new ones. We're going to need as many drawings as we can get."

"OK, Daddy," she answered coyly. "We'll see what we can negotiate."

That's my girl, he thought.

The next day, Paul was running a new set of numbers past Burton. "We've got to get the price down, Burton. Our production costs are just over a dollar per cookie. You're using a lot of high-end ingredients here; unfortunately, it *does* cost more to eat healthy. We've got to get the price point in line with school budgets. Right now, the cookies are going to be too pricey for a kids' snack."

"Well, remember, the idea is that these are more of a meal than a snack. I think a little over a dollar in ingredients isn't bad when you look at it as a complete meal," Burton said as he thumbed through Paul's report. "I'm sure Bob and Will can work on production costs. There must be a few things we can tinker with."

"Are you kidding?" Paul threw back. "Those two won't even *consider* using cheaper ingredients. We also have to stick to the federally approved ingredient list. No one wants to cut corners."

"I know. I don't either. The whole concept is about quality.

I don't want to compromise—especially before we've even started."

"I get that. But I also know, as it stands now, that we'd need to sell these at a price that's out of range for school kids."

Burton sat back in his chair. His shirtsleeves were rolled up and his top button was open. His tie was long abandoned. He pressed his hands together, sitting quietly. A long moment passed, and Paul began to shift uncomfortably in his seat. "Uh, Burton?"

"What if," Burton stood up and paced to the window, "we are looking at this the wrong way?"

"How else can you look at production costs? This is math, not magic."

"True." Burton looked at Paul with a grin. "Corporations give huge donations to charities every year. Companies are looking for ways to give back, to improve their communities. It's the triple bottom line—profit, plus environmental consciousness, plus social enhancement. What if business groups could 'adopt' schools? They'd have a local, hands-on opportunity to give, and kids would have a healthy meal option. I can think of a dozen CEOs who would love to do something like that."

"Are people really going to sponsor a meal cookie, Burton?"

"Yes! There is a chorus of people out there upset at the food served to kids. We know we need to change. Schools have a terrible time changing focus, and they're the ones that are supposed to be teaching these kids how to live better. It's a lumbering bureaucracy, but *we* can hustle. We can deliver something better. I think a lot of people will see the value in working on the problem together. It's the kind of social enterprise people can get excited about. It isn't just a check disappearing into the system; this is putting something warm and wholesome into the hands—no, the stomachs—of school kids." Burton felt more and more excited about this angle. He knew it could work.

Paul wasn't far behind. "Your idea of student artwork would fit right in. The sponsoring business could have its name on the wrapper, along with student artwork from the sponsored school."

"Exactly!" Burton was writing furiously. "It could work, Paul."

"This could be a lot of work. We need to really think this through. We also need to figure out if this could even be a possibility with most school districts. We need to see how open they are to corporate sponsors."

"They let in every company pushing fast food junk. I'd have a hard time believing they wouldn't be willing to work with a health food company and other companies that want to back such a positive initiative."

"That's true. My grandson smells like a pizza when he gets out of school." Paul began to write his own list of questions. The two men were silent as they each jotted notes.

Gail walked in with a fresh pot of coffee. "You two look serious," she said as she refilled their cups.

"I think we have an idea, Gail."

"What else is new? You've been churning out ideas for months. It's always something new with you," she smiled.

Always something new. That's music to my ears, Burton thought joyfully.

Burton and Paul shared their idea with Gail, their excitement and enthusiasm growing as they spoke. Gail, as a grandmother and active PTA member, more than validated the two men. She began brainstorming with them, eager to give her insight about schools and fundraising programs.

That night, after the dishes were done and the kids had gone up to their rooms, Burton and Julie sat at the kitchen table. Julie got up suddenly and left the room. She came back with a letter postmarked from Lost Hills and handed it to Burton. "This came for you today." She sat back down.

Burton flipped the envelope over a couple of times and then tore it open. He pulled out a single-page handwritten letter and started reading aloud. "Dear Mr. Hall. We received our second box of Hall's meal cookies this morning. I can't tell you how grateful I am for your kindness. My kids love the cookies—all 10 flavors. I understand you're working on getting them into schools. Well, I sure hope that works out, because their friends are awfully jealous, even though my kids are good at sharing! I've enclosed some pictures the kids drew for you. I guess they were inspired. Bless you, Mr. Hall." The letter was signed "Molly."

Burton pulled three neatly folded sheets of paper from the envelope. He opened them and laid them on the table so Julie could see them too. The first drawing was of a superhero wearing a cape. His one hand was raised to the sky in a fist, as though he was about to take flight. The other hand clutched a cookie. At the bottom, Ollie had written his name. The second drawing was of an angel. Simple, beautiful—though Burton noticed she had been drawn with a crooked halo. *Maybe that Rachel's a character*, he thought, smiling. Bobby's picture was of a boy playing basketball, but instead of a ball, he was using a giant meal cookie. "That's clever," said Julie, resting her hand gently on the paper.

Burton paused and fought back a tear and a large lump in his throat. "This is my landscape, Julie. Hugo was right—never give up," he whispered.

She got up again, left the room, and came back clutching

something in her hand. Then she went to the kitchen drawer and pulled out a pair of scissors. She laid the scissors on the table in front of Burton, and then a tie. It was bright pink and orange striped. Burton looked at Julie quizzically. "What's this about?" he asked.

"I'm asking you to step down as Mayor of Munchieville," she answered. "It's time for you to move out into the world."

"But Julie…" he began.

"No, Burton, let me finish. I love what we've built together, and I still need your help with the Miss Munchie line if you still want to be part of it. But I want you to know that you never have to wear that ridiculous tie again. Besides," she said with a little wave, "those definitely aren't your colors." She took Burton's hand across the table. "I believe in you, and in your dreams. I'm proud of you. And I'm behind you, always."

Burton looked at her for a moment, and then he ceremoniously snipped the tie right in half. He got up from his chair and pulled Julie to her feet to embrace her.

Chapter 16

We Have Liftoff

> Twenty years from now you will be more disappointed by the things that you didn't do than by the ones you did do. So throw off the bowlines. Sail away from the safe harbor. Catch the trade winds in your sails. Explore. Dream. Discover.
> —Mark Twain

OVER TWO MONTHS had passed since Burton received the green light from the state board of education to solicit corporate sponsors for the meal cookie program. He had been up and down the state making presentations and discussing the plan. Exhausted but still enthusiastic, he felt that the last few months had gone by quickly, and he was amazed at how far he'd come in such a short time.

Maximum Bob had worked up 10 different flavors of meal cookies, and there was something for everyone. They had kosher, vegan, and low-fat options—each with bright, colorful labels made by children. Now it was time to find the right sponsor and get the dream in motion.

KNEADING A DREAM

Burton pulled into the parking lot at the corporate headquarters of the largest gas company in the state. A sponsor of this size would definitely kick-start interest in the product. He took his box of samples and headed to the office of Maria Cruz, a public liaison supervisor who seemed really interested in the project.

"Ms. Cruz, Burton Hall," he said, extending his hand. "Thanks for meeting with me."

"My pleasure, Mr. Hall. Please sit down." She looked down at her notes. "So you are the cookie man."

Burton grinned and nodded, looking at his tie, printed with a tiny cookie pattern—a gift from Julie. "What was your first clue?"

"Let's go into the conference room. The group is ready for you." Maria escorted Burton into a large, sunny conference room. There were at least a dozen people sitting around the table. Burton noticed a tray of tired-looking bagels in the center.

"I have some samples for everyone to enjoy while I set up." Burton began to place his cookies, complete with the gas company logo on the wrapper, on a large tray. Feel free to help yourselves. We have many flavors available." The tray began to make its way around the group, and people began talking and sharing the cookies. By the time Burton had his presentation slides up and running, the room had erupted in an excited, animated chatter. The Doughgods were working their usual magic.

Maria drew the group's attention, introducing Burton as well as quieting them. "As you know," she began, "City Utilities, like so many large companies these days, is seeking opportunities to influence the community in a positive way. We want to build community partnerships. Our directive is to go beyond traditional marketing and look for ways to build an image that has real and enduring value for our customers. Mr. Hall has a program he has developed that provides a healthy snack to schoolchildren."

Burton began his presentation. When he finished, his audience burst into applause. Maria stood and turned to him. "After looking at the materials you sent earlier this week, I'd like to tell you that we are making a two-million-dollar commitment to the Hall's meal cookie program—sponsoring 23 elementary schools in our service area. We're excited to be one of your first partners, and we're sure this program will mean a lot to the schools and communities it serves." Burton was stunned. He knew the gas company was interested, but he never expected such a sizeable commitment right off the bat. Maria continued, "There are a few details to work out, but we're excited. This is exactly the kind of social-awareness project we were looking for. I hope you're ready to jump in and get started."

Burton smiled at Maria. "I am. I'd like to get my heart started again first, of course."

"Well, we'd like to have you sit with our corporate attorney and review a few things. That will either get your heart racing or put you into a coma."

"Be happy to." Burton watched the group file out, taking the remaining samples with them.

Epilogue

You may say I'm a dreamer, but I'm not the only one.
—John Lennon

BURTON AND JULIE stood on the fringes of the cafeteria, watching the children inhale their lunches—assorted varieties of Hall's newly dubbed "Mealies." The kids were talking with their mouths full and spilling a glass of milk here and there, but they were happy—and they were eating. The couple had stood there surveying the scene for about 15 minutes when Burton felt someone tap his shoulder. It was Mike Collier.

"Mike! Great to see you!" Burton pumped Mike's arm.

"It's great to see you too. I hear you've been busy lately."

"That's for sure. You could say I've been flying in friendlier skies." The men exchanged a knowing glance. Burton introduced Mike to Julie and then asked, "What are you doing here? This is a surprise, though I'm glad to see you."

"Your secretary said I'd find you here, and I think I'm about to make you *very* glad to see me," Mike said evasively.

Burton was curious, of course. "What are you talking about? Out with it!"

Mike nonchalantly handed Burton a folded piece of paper. Burton opened it to discover that it was a sizable check. He saw who it was from and nearly gasped. "What's this?" Burton was incredulous. "What's this about?"

Mike grinned like the Cheshire cat. "Well, you could say I still have some pretty powerful connections, but, better than that, you've got an amazing product to offer. They want to sponsor the program in 25 southern state schools. That check may be only the first of many."

Burton let out his breath. He was stunned. The check was from Brigham Air.

"Even better than that, my friend," Mike said, still grinning, "they want to talk to you about a version of your beloved meal cookie for air travel."

"What?" Burton was floored. "But what about Gary? What about...?"

"Remember our friend Morty?"

Burton just nodded, still stunned.

"Well," Mike continued, "the guy's a bit of a shark, but he's also got a lot of connections most people don't. He had a friend do some digging on our buddy Gary, and he was let go at Brigham for hammering out a few 'special favors' from their suppliers. He's done a lot of harm and taken a lot of people—you're not the first.

Burton was speechless for a moment. *Brigham Airlines wants my business.* It was unbelievable. *But what do I want?* He turned to Mike, "You know, if they're the kind of company that brings a guy like Gary onside, someone who would take another man's ideas and pass them off as his own, I don't think I want their business. I don't think I want their sponsorship either." He handed the check back to Mike.

"Hold on there, Burton," Mike said, looking him in the eye. "This is legit. Gary fooled Brigham Air, too. They had no idea he'd stolen anything at all. They trusted him, just like you did. Here," he continued, "Susan asked me to give you the check, but she wanted me to make sure you had this too." He pulled a bulky envelope from inside his jacket and handed it to Burton.

Burton opened the envelope. Inside was his diary. There was a slip of paper protruding from inside. The paper was marking the page where Burton had first recorded his airline idea. On it, Susan had written a short note: "I'm glad to return this to its rightful owner—and to the man with all the good ideas. Please be in touch."

"Well I'll be..." Burton was stunned.

Mike broke his reverie. "Burton, let them help you do this. They want in, with or without your business on top of it."

Burton let Mike give him back the check. "Thanks for looking out for me and for looking out for this idea. You've already done so much for me... Why'd you do this?"

Mike put his hands in his pockets and shifted his weight. "I guess I believed in what you were trying to do. And look at this!" he said, gesturing to the room of noisy kids. "You've outdone yourself."

"Well, I had plenty of help, yours included."

They were interrupted by a commotion behind them. A man had just come into the cafeteria, his arms weighed down by art supplies. It was Hugo. Burton turned and helped him empty his arms so he could give him a proper handshake. "Julie, Mike, this is my good friend Hugo."

Mike shook his hand. "I've heard so much about you," Julie said, extending her hand.

Burton helped Hugo set up his easel and found a hard-backed

chair to help him get comfortable. Both men had a twinkle in their eye. Burton rested his hand on Hugo's shoulder and turned to Mike and Julie. "Hugo here is a memory painter, and he's here to paint a memory today for me and the Special Kneads team. I asked him to come and paint this—this landscape," he pointed to the busy cafeteria. "My friends, this is what true success looks like. This is a landscape worth painting. After Hugo's finished, we're gonna auction it off at a corporate fundraising golf tournament we're having next month to sponsor more schools. I couldn't think of a better way to commemorate this day—and this dream."

Hugo looked at Burton, like a proud father would look at his son. "I'm glad to be here, Burton. Glad to see this day. Just keep dreaming those dreams, son. Dream those dreams."

And Burton knew he would.